SONS OF THE DARK

barbarian

LYNNE EWING

ATTENTION READER
This is an uncorrected galley proof. It is not a finished book and is not expected to look like one. Errors in spelling, page length, format, etc., will be corrected when the book is published several months from now. Direct quotes should be checked against the final printed book.

HYPERION/NEW YORK

 For information address Volo Books for Children, 114 Fifth Avenue, New York, New York 10011-5690.
First Edition
1 3 5 7 9 10 8 6 4 2
Printed in the United States of America
ISBN 0-7868-1811-5
Reinforced Binding
Library of Congress Cataloging-in-Publication Data on file.
Visit www.volobooks.com

For all the bad boys who told me their secrets: Victor Carrillo, Tom Cooper, Jonathan Fitz Gerald, Bob Gately, Kevin Gordon, Alex Morales, Marcos Morales, Jr., and Bill Savage.

PROLOGUE

361 A.D.

Lisha did not summon the midwife when the first labor pain pinched her back. Instead she fled her home and ran into the forest. It was risky to deliver the baby alone, but she had to keep the birth a secret to protect her child. She was a rune master, her powers strong but no match for her sister Shatri's dark sorcery.

The next contraction made her stop, and her uneasiness grew. She needed to hide, and quickly. She started walking again, but before long the evergreens and underbrush became impenetrable. She gathered fallen branches and, using a sharp rock, scratched delicate block letters into the bark. Flames burst from the inscription, and a crackling fire soon cut the cold damp. At last she lay back on the pine needles and waited.

Hours later Lisha cradled her son, but he had a warrior's lungs, and his cries stirred the night. The giant boughs rustled overhead, and Shatri appeared, her white fur cloak a radiant halo in the gloom. Blood-blackened runic symbols covered her staff. She lifted it and decreed that the baby would live for only as long as the fire burned.

Lisha vowed to make the blaze eternal and defiantly threw kindling onto the flames. Shatri laughed at her sister's effort and swept her staff toward the sky. Lightning flashed and rain burst from the clouds, drowning the fire. Trium-phant, Shatri stopped the storm and left.

The death-giving goddess Hel came for the child. But Lisha refused to let her infant son go motherless into death. She quickly worked a spell that tethered their souls: now one spirit could not be taken without the other.

The goddess admired Lisha's fierce love and gave her a choice; her child could live if she would commit him to the Four of Legend. Lisha knew the story well and, desperate to keep her son alive, agreed.

As soon as the goddess left, Lisha emptied her charm pouch. Small gray rune stones spilled onto the ash and, in the dim light from the embers, she studied the way the pebbles had fallen. The blank rune dominated the cast of stones; her son's fate could not be changed. Now she cursed her selfish love. In keeping her son alive she had bound him to a pitiless and immutable destiny.

CHAPTER ONE

THE HIGH SCHOOL campus was curiously quiet and deserted near the back of the gym. Even so, Obie shot a quick look over his shoulder before he ducked behind a Dumpster filled with foul-smelling banana peels and discarded sack lunches. He squeezed between a chain-link fence and the corner of the building. The wire mesh rattled and clanked against the metal posts, and the portable CD player in his hand scraped against the graffiti-covered wall. Once through, he followed a path around a pile of broken desks and old football sleds.

On the other side, students crowded a narrow corridor, clustered in small groups of two or three, and pinching cigarettes. Smoke scratched the inside of Obie's nose and throat and filled his mouth with a harsh tobacco taste.

"Hey." Obie nodded.

No one returned his greeting.

A girl grudgingly stepped aside and let him pass. Only losers hung out in Smoker's Alley, and the kids glaring at him now were proud to be the school's rock-bottom bad. Obie was unwelcome and could see the annoyance on their faces, but he stayed anyway. He felt safer among the unpopular. He didn't fit in at Turney High, and secretly he dreaded the day when he did, because that would mean he had given up.

He was a loner, and purposely so. It was too dangerous for him to get close to anyone—not that anyone had even tried until last week. Then everything had changed. His band Pagan had burned its first CD and all the Los Angeles rock stations were giving their songs airtime. The sudden success made his secret harder to hide. Saturday night, after the band had finished playing in a Sunset Strip rock club, some girl-fans had followed him back to the apartment where he lived with two other guys. What would have happened if the girls had seen him do something strange? He didn't need witnesses to add to his problems.

But he wasn't going to worry about that now. He was too anxious to hear the raw track of his new song. He slipped on his earphones, pressed the start button on his CD player, then slid it into his jacket pocket and closed his eyes. A four-chord slam of guitar music rushed into his head. The band might get some serious backing from a big label with this one, but money wasn't his thing. Music was.

He hummed the opening phrase. Then, without thought, his fingers attacked invisible strings and played the killer riff. The crushing thunder of drums joined the melody. Obie nodded with the beat, waiting for his cue, and then he sang along, his tone uninhibited and free. Rage at injustice powered his voice, and his lungs bled the raw angry words. Pain gave him inspiration. Pain gave him purpose. Pain sucked.

Time for his guitar solo, but before it

played, an unsettling shift in pressure jarred his concentration. His eyes flashed open, his muscles tensed, and his hands clenched, ready to fight, but no one stood near him. Still the peculiar sense of danger didn't go away. He tore off his earphones, and his long blond hair spilled over his jean jacket. He stuffed his headset into his pocket and glanced at the leaden sky. The air felt stagnant and eerily heavy.

"Freak," a girl whispered harshly. Stars and crescent moons were tattooed around her wrists like bracelets. She had been writing poetry on her boyfriend's back. Now she snapped the top back on to her purple felt marker and pulled his shirt down over her work. Her eyes never left Obie.

She wasn't the only one watching him. Kids stared anxiously, waiting to see what he was going to do next. They didn't seem to notice the subtle change in the air, and even if they had, they wouldn't have understood what it meant.

But the dead calm unnerved him, and his heart began to pound. Had someone found him after all? This tight passageway would be perfect for an ambush, but he had no intention of getting caught, not yet, anyway. Since arriving in Los Angeles three months ago, he had sensed danger, but this was the first time he had felt it so close.

A sound, low and barely audible, trembled through the stillness as if something invisible were coming toward him. Obie tensed. The parched grass rustled, and the white, puffball heads of dandelions released a snow of floating seeds, though the day was windless.

"Dude," a deep voice called.

Startled, Obie looked down.

Two guys in faded black concert tees were crouching nearby beneath a dry, dusty oleander bush. They were getting hammered on something in a brown paper bag.

"The Barbie girl is looking for you." The skinny one pointed, and his studded leather cuff slipped down his bone-thin arm. Obie frowned and turned.

Kirsten Ashton stood near the pile of discarded desks. She smiled and raised her hand in a silly wave. Her shining curls and glossy pink lips clashed with the stark black eyeliner, straight hair and major attitudes of the girls who hung out in Smoker's Alley. Her sudden appearance surprised him, but she couldn't have caused the odd feeling that someone had been nearby, watching him.

She clutched her notebook against her chest and moved softly through the weeds, waving hi to everyone she passed, oblivious to their cold, silent stares. She had the regal confidence of all popular kids and assumed she'd be accepted anywhere.

Kirsten stopped near Obie. "I called your name three times. Didn't you hear me?" she asked sweetly and cocked her head.

"No." Obie wondered what she wanted with him. She sat behind him in history class and was always acting as if he weren't even there. Not that he cared.

"I love your new song," she said with a flirty smile. "I heard 'Time Trap' on the radio this morning. It's going to be a big hit."

"Thanks," he said, concentrating on the

atmosphere; the feeling of alarm that had enveloped him moments ago had faded, but still he felt concerned.

"Your music makes me feel so much longing." She brushed a hand through her platinum-blond hair. The silver color on her fingernails matched her eyeliner. "Where do you get your inspiration?"

He shrugged, and before Kirsten could say more, the warning bell rang signaling the end of lunch. Kids stamped out their cigarettes and started back to class. Kirsten joined them, asking a girl with purple dreadlocks where she had purchased her chunky black boots.

But Obie didn't want to push in to the crush of kids sneaking back onto campus before the final bell. He charged off in the other direction and lunged between two overgrown Arizona cypresses. The scratchy branches snapped and cracked as he threw himself out on the other side. He wiped gluey cobwebs and needles from his face and hair, then sprinted across the basketball courts toward the front of the school.

He turned onto a breezeway and dodged

around kids hurrying to class. His boots pounded the concrete with a thumping noise louder than the rowdy yells and laughter. He took the next corner too quickly and slammed into Allison Taylor. She had been standing with her friends and now their circle broke apart, startled by his sudden appearance.

"Sorry." He caught Allison around the waist before she fell. Her dark hair swept over his chest, and her flowery perfume spun around him. He breathed in her fragrance like a thief, and let his hands linger on her soft, warm skin. She reminded him of someone he had known another time. "I didn't mean to knock you over," he said, apologizing.

Allison pulled back and looked down. "It's only a foot. I'll get a new one."

Her friends laughed.

She wore leather sandals, silver toe rings, and strings of beaded hemp around her thin ankles. A bruise was swelling on the top of her foot. He felt like whisking her into his arms and carrying her to one of the picnic benches in the quad to make sure she was okay, but he controlled the impulse; such things weren't done here.

Allison turned back to her friends as if Obie weren't even standing there.

"I just got a chill," Allison said and rubbed the gooseflesh on her tanned arms. "Someone must have walked over my grave."

"That didn't give you the chill," Obie said, intruding again.

Allison's friends stared at him. Arielle adjusted her halter as if Obie's presence had made her uncomfortable, and Caitlin tugged nervously at her earring, waiting to see what Allison would do.

"Are you telling me it was the thrill of seeing you?" Allison asked, breaking the tension.

Arielle laughed too loudly, and Caitlin continued to stare.

"As if." Allison rolled her eyes and turned away from him again.

Obie continued slowly down the outside corridor, kids shoving around him, to the other side of the classroom door, and settled back against the wall, alone. He watched Allison.

She was the most popular girl at John Turney High, and kids gathered around her as if she were a movie star handing out autographs. What would she have done if he had told her the true reason for her gooseflesh? He smirked, imagining her reaction, but in the end she wouldn't have believed him, and it would only have given her one more reason to make fun of him.

"She'll never go out with you," a sulky voice whispered. Kirsten stood beside him, spreading brown gloss onto her lips. He hadn't heard her sidle up next to him.

"Like I care," he answered back.

"Don't lie to me." Kirsten seemed annoyed. "Your crush is so obvious."

"Crush?" Obie stared at her.

"You're crushing on her bad," Kirsten explained. "Anyone can see you're crazy in like with her."

"You're wrong," he said, finally understanding her choice of words. "I don't like her." No girl was worth the risk. He couldn't change what fate had made him.

"Whatever," Kirsten said as if she didn't believe him. "Anyway it's a waste of time. Allison is totally into jocks, and now all your flirting has just made Sledge angry."

"I wasn't flirting." Obie followed her look.

Tony Sledgeheimer stood with Allison, leaning possessively over her. His broadness made her seem smaller. He was the Turney High quarterback. The *Los Angeles Times* sportswriters had nicknamed him "the Sledgehammer" because he could plow through the defensive line for a touchdown as easily as he could throw a long-bomb. Everyone said he'd be recruited by all the major colleges. But right now Sledge was glaring at Obie as if he wanted to execute a quarterback sneak and dive headfirst into Obie's chest.

Sledge walked over to Obie, rolling a comic book up tightly in his hand. He was extraordinarily good-looking. Three thin scars dimpled the skin under his left eye. He shaved his head, and his eyebrows were thick and perfectly shaped over intense, deepset eyes.

His best friends Barry and Forrest followed

after him like a wall. Forrest played right tackle for Sledge and maintained that position even off the field. Barry played center; he snapped the ball to Sledge and, so far this season, hadn't fumbled. He ran faster than either Sledge or Forrest and seemed smarter, too.

"Geez, you did it now." Kirsten inhaled sharply and eased away. "Someone get security," she said, to no one in particular.

"I saw you talking to Allison again," Sledge said and flicked the rolled-up comic in Obie's face. Anger blazed in his green eyes, and a red flush gathered around his ears. He folded his arms across his chest. Barbed-wire tattoos circled his biceps.

"And?" Obie remained slouched against the wall, indifferent to Sledge's threatening stance.

"You're such a wiseass," Forrest said. He stood to the right of Sledge, poised inches in front of him, his knuckles bruised and swollen from slamming his fists into face guards and shoulder pads. "Allison doesn't like you bothering her. Get it?"

"That's too bad." Obie grinned tauntingly. "I was thinking about asking her out."

Sledge tossed the comic book away and lunged toward Obie, but Forrest intervened, as if shielding Sledge from a defensive lineman.

"Everyone knows she belongs to Sledge," Forrest said and jerked a fat thumb back at Allison.

Forrest's choice of words triggered an ugly memory inside Obie. He squelched his urge to punch. He didn't need another trip to the V.P.'s office. "You might terrorize the rest of the school, but I'll talk to Allison whenever I want. She doesn't belong to anyone."

Barry lifted his calculus book threateningly, and the lines deepened across his forehead. His neck was thick and sunburned. "She's going with Sledge."

"I can't explain her bad taste," Obie answered.

"What are you thinking, punk?" Sledge drew closer, his chest touching Obie's.

Instead of feeling intimidated, Obie felt suddenly calm; he loved to fight. "I'm thinking you're standing this close because you want to dance with me," Obie said, goading.

Sledge swung his fist in answer but Obie caught his wrist. Forrest cursed and plowed Obie into the wall, but the tackle wasn't enough to make Obie loose his grip.

"What's with you?" Barry dropped his book with a loud *thwack* and lumbered forward. His clenched hand came down, aimed at Obie's head, but Obie thrust his arm up as if he bore a shield and deflected the blow.

Sledge grabbed at Obie's fingers, trying to free his wrist.

"Good morning, students." Mr. Guzman's happy voice stopped the assault.

Barry and Forrest turned away, smiling broadly, as if the confrontation had been a playful skirmish. Barry even patted Obie's back as a good friend might do, then gathered his math book and the homework pages scattered over the walk and started toward class.

"It's over now," Sledge said and tried to wrench himself free, but Obie didn't release him.

"You're not so tough," Obie whispered and

held on long enough to let Sledge know that he had won, then let go.

"Later." Sledge picked up his comic book, then stood and stared fiercely at Obie. "You're in it deep now."

Obie snickered. "You don't even know what trouble is. You don't have a clue." Sledge looked at him oddly, his mind trying to work around the words, then followed the others into class.

At last Obie went in. He plopped down into his seat up front, near Mr. Guzman's desk and ignored the stares and whispers.

Forty-five minutes later, Obie sat restlessly, his feet stretched out under the teacher's desk. A dull ache had started to pound across his forehead, and Kirsten sat behind him, annoyingly braiding and unbraiding his hair.

"The Visigoths believed the dead person was still alive and lived on in the grave, suffering from cold, wet, hunger, and thirst." Mr. Guzman stood in front of the class, repeatedly tapping the chalk against the timeline he had drawn on the board.

School was different here. Obie liked physics, but history bored him, because so much of it was wrong. A red book on Mr. Guzman's desk caught his eye. He read the words on the spine, *The History of the Goths.* Obie leaned forward and took the book. Mr. Guzman glanced at him but didn't appear to object. Obie thumbed through the index, looking for a reference to King Filimer. He found one and turned to the page. The lecture became a low, humming backdrop as he read.

"Mythical!" he whispered and a terrible loneliness spread through him. After all the king's great battles and deeds, history had declared him unreal!

"Obie, maybe you have something you'd like to add to what I've been saying," Mr. Guzman said.

Obie looked up. Muffled laughter came from the back of the room.

"I was explaining the belief system of the Visigoths before they came in contact with the Christians." Mr. Guzman stepped closer, sniffed, then examined Obie's eyes, his way of testing for drugs. "Perhaps you could add something. What did the Goths believe happened after death?"

Kids in the back snickered. Someone whispered, "Stoner."

Obie broke out in a cold sweat.

"Well?" Mr. Guzman took back the book, carefully keeping it open to the page Obie had been reading. "We're all waiting."

"The dead keep in touch with the living," Obie blurted out, and he rushed on, "so they can warn their family, or the ones they love, if something bad is going to happen in the future. And they defend their burial mound against grave robbers, and sometimes they terrorize their enemy as a *draugr*."

Mr. Guzman stared at him, speechless. Finally, he spoke. "*Draugr?*" Mr. Guzman pronounced the word wrong.

Obie cleared his throat. "The living dead."

Silence ticked around him. He felt everyone staring at him. He was grateful when the bell rang.

Kids closed their books and started

crowding toward the door. Sledge strolled past Obie and gave him a piercing stare. Forrest and Barry bumped into his desk, sending the metal legs screeching across the linoleum into the teacher's desk. Mr. Guzman looked up, frowning.

"Excuse me," Forrest shouted with exaggerated politeness. "I tripped."

Then he and Barry laughed, tumbling against each other, and followed Sledge outside.

Obie walked down the corridor, bumping into other students, and staring at the runic inscription he had written on his wrist. The inscription was one he had written to protect himself. He cut across the empty stretch of pavement filled with picnic tables where kids sat and ate their lunches.

He sighed. He'd had enough of school for one day and decided to leave. He was hurrying across the quad and racing toward the front gate when an odd feeling swept over him again. He turned to find the source, and when he breathed again, his lungs were filled with the unmistakable odor of a hot summer day, even though cool air still rose from the concrete beneath his feet. A haunting melody whispered to him. He had heard that wind song only once before, on a sunless day like this one, and now he felt intense longing for home, but was helpless to return to his family.

Against his will, his mind floated back to the memory of warriors slipping silently through the tall spikes of sedge grass. He and his father had watched their vast clan of Visigoths cross the marshland, the smells of leather, horses, and blood heavy in the sultry heat.

The day had started out with pride and had ended with victory, the warriors proclaiming themselves a race of gods and heroes. Women and children had gone into battle with the men and, with triumphant cries, had shared the glory.

Obie stood motionless now, the battle stench rising in his nostrils, reviving the memory of the best and worst day of his life. His father had been murdered that hot afternoon, and now Obie wondered if the ones who had killed his father had finally found a way to travel through time and come for him, the only surviving son of the Gothic king Filimer, hidden seventeen centuries away.

CHAPTER TWO

BY LATE AFTERNOON the sun had burned away the cloud cover, and heat had settled on the day, heavy and smog-laden. Obie walked down Hollywood Boulevard, breathing in the metallic air. Maybe the suffocating heaviness he had felt at school had only been a strange mix of homesickness and pollution and not, as he had imagined, something moving toward him through time.

A lazy breeze rustled the palm trees, and spiky shadows flickered over the tourists as they crowded around the pink granite stars. Obie stepped carefully around them. The first time he had seen the Walk of Fame he had thought the sidewalk was a cemetery, and the bronze medallions, headstones.

The door to Musso and Frank's grill opened, and the savory smells of roast beef, garlic, and onions drifted around Obie. His stomach rumbled. He hadn't eaten lunch because he needed every penny for the amp he was picking up.

A few blocks later, he entered Beckman Guitar Shop. He carefully twisted around displays of strings, accessories, used guitars, and amplifiers. Stacks of sheet music and CDs crowded the shelves. An orange flyer, advertising his band's performance tonight, was tacked on a bulletin board behind a dusty cash register.

He pushed past a dirty red curtain into a backroom lit with fluorescent lights. The air smelled of contact cleaner, burning insulation, and lilac perfume.

Dahlia looked up and smiled. A dozen silver hoops pierced her ears. She turned off her soldering torch, lifted her safety glasses, and wiped her hands on her oversize apron.

"Hey, Obie. Your amp's done." She lifted a battered black box with chrome corners.

"I replaced the knobs, nulled the tin sounds like you asked, and added a tube," Dahlia said.

"Will it work with other speakers?" Obie asked. The band already had a great Marshall Stack, amplifiers and speakers, but Obie needed something deeper, with a different tone.

"Definitely," Dahlia answered and unsnapped the clasps on the guitar case. She took out the most beautiful guitar Obie had ever seen. A dragon's head covered the body. She handed it to him. "Here, try it out with my guitar."

"Are you sure you want me to play it?" Obie asked, and ran his fingers over the smooth cherrywood neck. "It looks expensive."

"Sure. Somebody should use it," Dahlia said. "It was a gift from my daughter's father."

"I didn't know you had kids." Obie strapped on the guitar. His conversations with Dahlia had always been about guitars, amps, and music.

"My daughter turned sixteen last month." Dahlia attached the cable to the guitar; she plugged it into Obie's amp, turned the controls, and nodded.

Obie tried one note. The tone was pure, deep, and haunting. His heart pounded, and he shot through a riff. The sound was powerful. He smiled.

"I told you I could do it," she said proudly. "No volume increase. Just boom."

"Thanks." Obie played a little more, then carefully handed the guitar back to her. He pulled a wad of bills from his back pocket and started counting them into a stack on the bench.

Dahlia stopped him. "You don't need to pay me all at once. Just a little at a time."

She took a twenty off his pile and stuffed it into her apron pocket. "This is enough for now. You keep the rest and give me more later."

He hesitated.

"I know you can't afford it," she said softly.

"Thanks, Dahlia. I'll pay you. I promise."

"I know you will," she said, ignoring his gratitude as if it embarrassed her. "How are you going to get the amp home?" She turned down the master volume, then unplugged the cord and set the guitar back in its case.

"I was going to grab a cab," Obie lied. He

couldn't tell her how he really planned to take the amp home.

"My daughter's upstairs," she said, already starting up the stairs to the apartment above. "She can give you a ride. She's so excited about having a driver's license, she'll be happy for an excuse to drive."

While he waited, Obie walked around the room, reading the autographs on the posters of the rock stars hanging on the wall.

At last footsteps pounded on the stairs again. Obie glanced up. Dahlia returned. Allison followed behind her.

"Allison?" Obie said, startled.

Allison took one look at Obie and stopped. A camera hung around her neck. She wore a halter top and low-slung shorts; her skin glistened, and she smelled of suntan oil. Her shoulders had started to burn, giving her a deep, brown-red glow.

Obie tried to stay focused on her face, but it was hard to keep his eyes from wandering, and then he caught her sullen stare. She didn't appear happy to see him.

"She was up on the roof, taking candid snaps of tourists with her zoom lens." Dahlia paused, suddenly noticing the tension in the air. "Do you two know each other?"

"We're in the same world history class," Allison offered glumly.

"Dahlia's your mom?" Obie said, incredulously. He cleared his throat and tried again. "I mean Mrs. Taylor is your mother?"

"We don't have the same last name." Allison scowled, as if daring him to say something. Her lips pinched tightly around her words. "I'm Taylor. She's Beckman."

"I didn't marry Allison's father." Dahlia seemed okay with sharing this bit of family history with Obie, but Allison clenched her teeth, seeming rankled at her mother's confession.

Obie glanced at one of the posters on the wall. "Your father is—"

"You ready?"

"Sure." Obie picked up the stack of money.

Allison glared pointedly at the bills, and angrily snapped the lens cap onto her camera.

She reached around him, heat radiating from her sun-soaked body, and grabbed her car keys. She jingled them impatiently. "Let's go, then."

A buzzer sounded, and Dahlia started for the front of the store. "Good luck at the concert tonight, Obie," Dahlia said and pushed through the curtains.

"I don't know why you had to taunt Sledge today," Allison said as soon as her mother left them alone. "He's in enough trouble without you trying to goad him into another fight. He's got to have good citizenship to play on the team."

"He wouldn't have bothered me if you hadn't complained to him," Obie said, defending himself. "I bumped into you accidentally."

"I didn't say anything. I can take care of myself," Allison said. "It was Arielle and Caitlin. You freak them out, and just about everybody else at school."

Obie wondered if that were true. He stuffed the money in his back pocket, then lifted the amp and followed Allison down a wide, dim hallway to another door. She opened it, and a hot breeze blew over them, and then she turned to him, her hair cascading over her shoulders.

"Just so it's clear," she said, poised at the door. "I want you to know I don't promote wannabes the way my mother does, and I don't approve of her doing so, either."

"If this is about the money—" Obie started.

"Do you think you're the first guy my mother has given a loan?" Allison interrupted. "She helps every loser with a guitar."

"But I—"

"You won't pay the money back," Allison said bitterly, as if her mother had made a lot of bad loans in the past.

"I—" He tried to speak again, but Allison was too quick.

"And don't tell me you will," she went on. "No one ever has."

"I will," he said.

She looked at him sideways and gave him a skeptical squint. "I hate guys who want to be rock stars. They're self-centered and—"

His anger finally burst through. "Maybe

you just can't stand someone who's more interested in music than in you," Obie cut in angrily. He wanted to add more but held back. He had seen her at school. She was spoiled and used to being the center of attention.

Red spots flared on her tanned cheeks and she drew back, half hidden behind the door. "I just remembered my car's in the shop," she said, blatantly lying. Her Toyota was parked in a slot near the building. "I guess I can't give you a ride home after all. Sorry."

"I never asked for a ride in the first place," he said and adjusted the weight of the amp. "Your mother offered."

"Whatever." Allison tossed him a spiteful grin and closed the door.

"You know what caused that chill you felt today?" Obie yelled, anger and frustration making him reckless with his words. He wanted to tell her the truth and shake up her perfect life. Maybe fear would make her less arrogant. Then adrenaline rushed through him as the full impact of what he had just said hit him. What would he do if she opened the door to hear his explanation? He couldn't tell her. He'd have to lie.

But her response was the unmistakable snap of a dead bolt sliding into place.

"Just as well," Obie muttered, wondering why her dismissal hurt so deeply. It wasn't as if he could ever get involved with her. He heaved the amp onto his shoulder, and started walking, his eyes searching, looking for the right blend of shade in which to hide. He wondered what she would have done if he had told her the truth. Another universe paralleled modern-day Los Angeles, and for a nanosecond earlier today something in that world had collided with her, giving her the goose bump chill. Mostly, the boundaries between the two dimensions were solid, but sometimes a weakening occurred. The other realm also explained why people sometimes stumbled for no reason, or caught movement in the corner of their eye when nothing was there.

Obie knew because he was a Renegade, a fugitive from Nefandus where he had been a slave, a *servi*. Bounty hunters were trailing him, trying to capture him and take him back, but being hunted wasn't the worst of what was wrong with his life. When he had escaped, he had assumed he would go back to his own time and place, and find himself again in the forest and marsh lands of the Goth tribes living between the Rhine and Danube Rivers in the area today called Germany. Instead he had landed in twenty-first century Los Angeles. Now he was trapped more than sixteen hundred years from home.

Every day was a struggle for him, trying to fit into a world in which he didn't belong. He hated it here. He had studied the earth realm. Everyone in Nefandus had, including the *servi*, preparing for the day Nefandus invaded and took over the world of light. But even with an understanding of life here, he felt uncomfortable. More than anything he wanted to return to his own time before things had gone bad, but until he found a way, he had to make do here. If he hadn't heard an electric guitar playing hard rock blues his first day out, he probably would have returned to Nefandus, even with its danger and forced servitude.

He still didn't understand why he hadn't escaped to his own time. From the book he had read he knew it was possible. He paused, wondering how he could endure an earthbound eternity here. His master, Crowley Hawkwick, had made him immortal so he would remain frozen forever with the strength and energy of his fifteen years. But unlike the Immortals, Obie didn't have the power to regenerate. No slave had that ability. It hadn't concerned him then, because he had thought that when he came back to earth's realm, he would become mortal again. He had learned that wasn't true his first day out.

Dominique, another *servi*, had escaped with him. They had entered Los Angeles on Alameda Street near the train station. Obie had been cautious, but Dominique hadn't understood the danger in the truck speeding toward him. Sunlight had flashed off the chrome grill, blinding him, and he had been too stunned to move. The Mack truck had hit him before Obie could rescue him.

That was the day Obie had learned that

there were things worse than death. Dominique couldn't die. He had continued to exist, a bloodied mess of bone and skull. Obie had cradled Dominique's broken body, and together they had faded to shadow. Both of them were shape-changers. All *servi* could dissolve to darkness and float away. That had been the mode of transportation in Nefandus.

Together they had spun about, gazing at their strange new world, but eventually Dominique had pulled away, deciding to return to Nefandus, his decision unthinkable to Obie, but what else could he have done?

Now Obie entered a gloomy stairwell and started to dematerialize. It would be easier carrying the amp home, if both he and it were no more than a smudge of dark speeding across the shadows. But the sound of a door opening made him stop. He abruptly stepped back into sunlight as if he were going to Hollywood Boulevard to catch a cab.

"Come on back," Allison called petulantly. "Mom said I have to give you a ride home."

"Forget it," Obie shouted, reluctant to go

with her now. It was hot and he wanted to get back to the apartment, eat, take a shower, and try out the amp

The car engine as Allison's Toyota inched along beside him.

"Get in, please," she said through the open driver-side window and gave him a pretty smile. "I won't be able to go out tonight unless I take you home."

His shoulders slumped.

"Thanks," she said, in a throw-away expression of gratitude, as if she were used to getting her way. She set the brake, got out and helped him put the amp on the back seat. Then she slid behind the steering wheel again.

He climbed into the car, and she hit the accelerator before he had even put on his seat belt. The car jerked forward. She turned in to a side street, then yanked the steering wheel to the left and drove onto Hollywood Boulevard. She switched lanes and eased into the stop-and-go movement on Vine without saying a word. The traffic light turned red, and they stopped in front of Hollywood High.

"Why don't you go to school there?" Obie asked, looking at the mural of the famous alumni.

Allison leaned forward and snapped on the radio. Music blasted from the car speakers, making the dashboard vibrate, and ending any likelihood of conversation.

The green light came on, and the car chugged forward. A muggy breeze blew through the air vent, bringing a dank smell that reminded Obie of damp forest soil. The scent triggered a memory. He tried to push it back. It wasn't as if remembering could change where he was now. But the recollection came anyway, and in his mind's eye he was a small boy sitting with his mother again. She had shaken out the small leather pouch she always carried with her, and small gray stones had tumbled onto the forest floor.

Each day she had spent time with him, passing on the sacred knowledge of the runes. She had cautioned him to listen well as she described the purpose of each letter. She taught him the ancient alphabet, telling him that the letters were used for poetry, inscriptions, and divination, but that they were never spoken aloud carelessly; there was too much power in each letter's sound. He remembered the touch of his mother's lips against his hair, whispering the sound of each letter, as if saying them too loudly might release a terrible power.

The Toyota slowed, and the change in speed pulled him from his thoughts. He wondered what would happen if he called the sound of one letter now, or let an incantation tumble from his mouth. He hadn't tried in so long. His mother had died when he was eleven, her rune stones buried with her. Obie had forgotten much of what she had taught him, except for the one spell she had cast almost daily to make him tell her the truth.

He smiled now and glanced at Allison. She scowled unhappily at the glare reflecting from the car's hood, and before he could think it through, the words trembled on his tongue. A soft sound murmured, a power of its own, and pushed out through his lips. *"Du miht wip."* The air glowed briefly, and the sweet scent of burning roses that he remembered from his childhood filled the air.

Allison glanced at him, blinked and wiped her face, then smiled and turned off the radio. "I'm sorry about all that back there." She bit her lip, then guardedly spoke, the hurt unmistakable in her voice. "My dad's other kids go to Hollywood High. I don't like running into them. That's why I go to Turney. I can't get used to the way my dad has abandoned me. I mean, he gives me everything but time. I was upset because he'd canceled another weekend visit. I'm normally not such a total bitch."

"It's all right," he said, and studied her closely.

"It's *not* all right," she answered, but then she stopped, and confusion crossed her face. "I don't know what made me tell you that. I haven't even told Sledge about my dad. It's a secret, all right?"

She moved the car to the side of the street and parked. "Maybe you should get out here," she said without explanation, but he sensed her embarrassment. She acted as if she were uncomfortable that she had told him her deepest secret.

He hesitated. His mother had explained the dangers of casting a spell without careful thought. He had been careless, and now he hoped he hadn't bound Allison to always telling the truth. He couldn't leave her until he knew it was only a temporary effect.

"Do you want to come to the concert tonight?" he asked, testing.

She looked at him oddly, as if he were offering her a dead snake. "I'd love to," she answered, in an obvious lie. "But I have plans already."

He smiled, satisfied the spell had only been temporary, and climbed out. He got his amp from the back. "Thanks for the lift."

She waved, and the Toyota took off with a muffled growl, as if she were anxious to get away from him.

He stared after her, the amp resting heavily against his chest. Then he walked down the street, past jewelry stores and pastry shops. Windows displayed Chinese imports: teas, fans, and red silks. Bins of ginseng, ginger, dried mushrooms, and shrimp lined the entrances, and different dialects, Cantonese and Mandarin, melodiously filled the air.

Obie started to think about the refrigerator in the loft, and hoped there was something left in it to eat, but suddenly, in spite of the a merciless sun, he felt a cold ripple, like a winter wind, cross his neck. He spun around, grasping the amp tightly, and caught something in his peripheral vision.

A shadow darted into a shop. The dark shape could have been a trick of light, caused by the glare from passing cars, but the swift movement seemed out of step with the crowded street and slow-moving traffic.

But maybe the shadow had been a *venator*, a bounty hunter, the worst kind of *servi*, one granted freedom to come and go between both worlds in order to capture Renegades and take them back to Nefandus. Bounty hunters had the power to change into shadowy apparitions, but so did he. Maybe Master Hawkwick had hired bounty hunters to bring him back. Yet he didn't understand why Hawkwick would want him back. Obie had no special knowledge, or power, like some *servi*, and he felt certain his master could easily replace him.

He walked back and looked into the shop where he thought he had seen the shadow. A woman eating rice with chopsticks stared back at him. He didn't see anything unusual, but his heart hammered as if his body sensed danger. He turned back to the street, and walked slowly through the throng of shoppers. Strange shapes hovered beneath the upturned eaves of a pagoda, giving the impression of faces. Was it only a mirage created by intense sunlight and heat, or were shape-shifters hiding there, watching him?

At the next corner, he ducked around the building and into a small grocery store. Two giant stone Foo dogs guarded the entrance against evil spirits. Obie stood stock-still and waited impatiently between huge sacks of rice. He peered out at the street. He had no intention of starting anything, but he wanted to see if anyone were really following him.

Seconds ticked by, and then he heard a fist-pounding beat. He realized his mistake; he should have stayed on the main street in the safety of the crowd. Now he was trapped.

CHAPTER THREE

BARRY'S HONDA SHRIEKED around the corner, slammed on its brakes, and skidded to a stop in front of Obie. Sledge turned down the thundering music and leaned out the passenger-side window. "We got you now, stoner."

Even from this distance, Obie could smell the sour stench of stale beer wafting from the car's interior. He didn't have time for Sledge's pathetic threats, and there was no way he was going to fight all three of them and risk damaging his amp. He looked for a way to escape, but no matter which way he went he couldn't outrun a car.

"You're caught," Sledge said and started to

get out. "We want you to take a little ride with us."

Forrest laughed from the backseat. "Yeah, we're just going to cruise around the 'hood." He finished his beer, crumpled the can, and tossed it out the window.

Obie took one step forward as if he were going to get into the car, but instead he whipped around and bolted into the shop. He raced down a narrow aisle and prayed there was an exit in the back.

The edge of his amp caught a pile of polished woks, and the aluminum cooking pans clattered to the floor. He jumped over one, and the weight of the amp threw him off balance. He knocked into a display of imported black teas. The gaily painted red-and-black tin boxes crashed around him and scattered noisily across the floor.

Someone shouted, "Earthquake!" But the clerk behind the counter must have seen Obie on a closed-circuit TV. He raced toward the back, trying to catch him. "What are you doing?" he yelled, stopping behind a barricade of onions and potatoes.

"I'll pay for it all. I promise," Obie yelled and squeezed between two aquarium tanks. He pushed under a curtain, ran through the kitchen, kicked open the back door, and fell into the blinding sunlight.

He stumbled, then caught himself and continued jogging, his boots slipping on the white gravel. The amp jostled painfully against his chest. He came to an intersection and had no idea which way to turn. He chose right and sprinted into a small parking lot behind a live-poultry store. The unpleasant smell of chickens filled the air, and each step kicked up a new flurry of feathers. He turned around and stopped, defeated. He had nowhere left to run.

Behind him a car engine revved, accelerating wildly, the tires crunching the loose rocks. The Honda would bear down on him in seconds. He had only moments to make up his mind. Kyle had warned him not to use his powers, but a fight didn't make sense. He didn't mind a bruise or even a broken bone, but he wanted to protect his amp. He was a shape-shifter. He could fade into shadow and become a ripple of floating shade.

The car raced toward him between the buildings, its chrome bumper reflecting a brilliant shaft of sunlight.

Without another thought, Obie leaned against the shady wall behind him and let his body darken like a sky fading to twilight. The amp lost color and seemed to wilt, melting into his arms. Obie's heartbeat slowed, and he spread like an eerie black mist across the bricks, and then his dim spectral form levitated, slipping slowly up the side of the building.

The Honda roared to a stop, spraying gravel.

Sledge and Forrest jumped out.

"Where is he?" Sledge demanded.

Barry climbed from the car and joined them. He flipped his sunglasses up onto his forehead and rubbed his eyes.

Obie materialized on the rooftop, near the condenser for the air conditioner. Still feeling boneless and less than solid, he glanced over the edge, watching Barry, Forrest, and Sledge wander about looking for him.

Without warning, Barry glanced up as if he had sensed Obie staring down at him. "There!" Barry shouted and pointed.

"How the—" Forrest started; then he whipped his head around and back again. "It's physically impossible. There's no fire escape, no ladder."

Sledge nudged him, annoyance on his face. "He's not Superman. There's got to be a door someplace, or at least a ladder. We'll find it." He started to walk along the wall as if he expected a stairwell to appear magically.

"It's only one story up," Forrest said, tromping behind Sledge. "Maybe he scaled the bricks like a rock climber."

"With that box he was carrying?" Sledge asked.

Barry glanced left and right, then squinted and stared back at Obie, a strange look of awe on his face.

"There's no door, man," he said with certainty. "No ladder. No way. And even if there was a ladder, he couldn't have gotten up there that quickly. We would have seen him."

"What do you mean?" Sledge asked.

"Read your comic books," Barry said. It sounded like a dismissal, but Obie knew it wasn't. Sledge devoured stories about superheroes and ordinary kids with mysterious powers.

Obie and Barry stared at each other, and an odd moment of mutual recognition passed between them. Barry shielded his eyes from the glaring sun and continued to gaze up, a strange smile curling on his lips. He had a hungry look. Obie sensed that Barry had been waiting a long time to find something he couldn't explain with science. Obie thought to cast a spell for forgetfulness, but he couldn't remember the incantation, or even if one existed. He wished now that he had listened more closely to his mother, or had at least tried to retain what she had told him.

"Come down," Barry said, speaking deliberately slow and loud as if he wanted to make sure Obie understood his words. "We won't hurt you. I promise. I just want to know how you got up there."

Obie stepped away from the ledge, the amp's weight suddenly unbearable. He stood in the shade cast by a humming compressor, safely out of view from anyone below, and slowly evaporated. A breeze lifted his shadow straight up, and he curled, like a trail of smoke. He tried to fix his mind around the look on Barry's face and the way he had wanted to talk. Did that mean he had seen Obie fade? What would happen now?

CHAPTER FOUR

OBIE HOVERED NEAR the ground, phantomlike, in the shade of a bougainvillea, its bright fuchsia flowers fluttering around him. A woman walked quickly by, her overstuffed shopping bag brushing through him. When he was certain no one had seen him, he pulled his nebulous shape into a dark silhouette. His feet became solid first, precariously balanced on knotted roots.

He juggled the amp and stepped to the entrance of the apartment building where he lived with two other guys, Berto and Kyle, Renegades like himself. When he'd moved in, Kyle had told him to tell everyone that he lived there with his father, but so far no one had bothered to ask. Unlike Kyle, Obie wasn't concerned about keeping up the lie. He didn't plan on staying in L.A. that long, especially now. His thoughts turned back to Barry. Maybe Obie had misunderstood his look.

Obie pressed the button for the elevator. The heavy metal door slid open, and he stepped into the cage that had been used when the building had still been a mill. The dome window at the top cast lifeless milky light.

The elevator stopped with a bump on the top floor and Obie stepped onto the landing. He juggled the amp, took a key from his pocket, slipped it into the lock, and opened a huge metal door.

Inside, large windows reached to the high ceiling and sunlight spilled across the concrete floor. Kyle was a student at Turney High and also an artist, and the smells of linseed oil, turpentine, and gesso, mixed oddly with the spicy fragrances from the Chinese and Vietnamese restaurants below.

Obie went into his room, bare of furniture

except for a mattress on the floor. Rumpled clothes were scattered about, tossed carelessly over books on football that he had checked out from the L.A. library this week. He hadn't understood the sport but liked the roughness of it and wanted to play. He set the amp next to an electrical outlet, anxious to try it out with his own guitar.

A clatter came from the kitchen. Obie hoped Berto was home, and not Kyle. He left his room and walked across the huge, open room. Drop cloths covered the unfinished floor. An easel stood in the corner near the window. Obie glanced at the canvas and instantly recognized the oddly perched balconies, hanging askew on the tall, narrow buildings. Kyle painted scenes of Nefandus for money. Art dealers loved the surreal look, and he had sold several to art shops in Hancock Park and Brentwood, but Obie worried about Kyle's odd attachment to a place better forgotten. What drew him back?

Kyle had been a slave in Nefandus, and like all *servi* he had been given immortality, not as a gift, but because slaves were more valuable if they remained young forever. Unlike Obie and Berto, though, Kyle had been able to escape after only two months of captivity and had succeeded In making it back to his own time. He claimed a monk had helped him leave, but Obie hadn't decided yet if he believed Kyle.

Obie stepped around the glass-brick wall into the kitchen. Kyle stood motionless in front of a seascape, staring at it as if he were looking at the real ocean. He was wearing slouchy jeans and a ripped tee. He seemed unaware that Obie had come in.

But then he spoke. "Why did you pick a fight with Sledge and his crew?"

"I didn't." Obie stared at Kyle's back and slid his hand over the smooth gray countertop.

"Even the stoners were talking about you today," Kyle said. "What made you charge through those old cypress trees?"

"I wanted to get away," Obie said. "What was wrong with that?"

Kyle turned, as if he were coming out of a creepy trance, and for a moment Obie thought he'd been crying. Slashes of brown-red paint covered the front of his T-shirt. He wiped his eyes, then raised an eyebrow. "A normal kid couldn't have broken through the branches. You had to have turned to shadow halfway through."

Obie grinned. "Maybe I faded a little."

"If you're not careful we'll have Social Services snooping around, and someone is bound to discover we're living alone without adult supervision. Maybe fifteen was considered a man in your time, but in Los Angeles the law says you're still just a kid. Do you want to end up in a foster home? Or maybe you'd like to be farmed out to some group home for 'at-risk youths'?"

"Sorry." Obie's throat tightened. He hated the way Kyle tried to control him and tell him what to do. He glanced at the kitchen, remembering it was his day to clean. Plastic mugs and plates were piled in the sink, pans littered the stove, the floor hadn't been swept for a week. Bags of trash sat in a heap, giving off a putrid smell. Obie didn't share Kyle's distaste for cockroaches; a few bugs didn't bother him, but maybe if he started picking up, it would get Kyle off his back. He turned the faucet, and hot water ran into the sink.

"Dishes can wait." Kyle turned off the water. "Rumors are spreading around school about you. Kids are getting nervous about your behavior. If one of them complains to his parents, and his parents call the school, that's it. The district has a zero-tolerance policy for drugs and violence, and you'll be investigated. You might even have to see a shrink."

Obie glanced at the words Kyle had taped onto the refrigerator and cupboard doors to help him understand slang. He had studied languages in Nefandus, and knew several, but that hadn't prepared him for the odd use of English in L.A. At last he found *shrink* and read the meaning.

"So what?" Obie opened the refrigerator and wondered what Kyle would do when he found out about his latest run-in with Sledge. "I don't care what the kids at Turney think of me. I didn't want to go to school, and I'm not going to waste time trying to fit in," Obie said. He pulled out a pack of hamburger meat and slammed the refrigerator door. "I just want to return to my own home."

"You can't go back," Kyle argued, frustration rising in his voice. "I wish you'd just forget about it and try adjusting to *this* world."

"Easy for you to stay," Obie countered and tore the plastic shrink wrap from the meat. "You're from this time."

"Just cooperate, all right?" Kyle pleaded. "It was your idea to put yourself out there and play in a band. I tried to talk you out of it." Kyle paused long enough for Obie to argue, but when he didn't, Kyle went on. "We need to live low-key here and not draw attention to ourselves, but now that you're becoming a rock star—"

Obie smiled; everyone thought it was about fame, but it was the music.

"It's going to be harder. What if they ask the band to go out on tour?" Kyle shook his head. "You can't do it unless you learn how to hide your freaking abilities, not flaunt them."

"No one has seen me do anything," Obie said. He wasn't entirely sure, though—what had Barry seen? He dug into the hamburger and tossed it into his mouth.

"Like that." Kyle cringed. "We don't eat raw meat. You have to cook it first."

"It tastes good." Obie popped another bite into his mouth.

Kyle turned away as if Obie were making him ill. Obie glanced at him, suddenly wondering if something more were bothering Kyle. "Did something happen to you?"

"I saw a bounty hunter," Kyle said, accusingly. "We've had more than our share of run-ins with *venatores* since you came."

"I haven't done anything to make bounty hunters come after me," Obie said. "You should be worried about Berto, not me. He disappears for days. Where does he go? Back to Nefandus? Maybe he upset someone and that's why so many hunters have come looking for us."

Kyle didn't look convinced, but before he could say more, the roar of Berto's motorcycle interrupted them. Kyle glanced at the clock.

"I'd better get ready for work." Kyle worked as an extra in movies, and was forever trying to get a speaking part.

Kyle started for his room, but paused and leaned back around the glass-brick partition. "You're sure you don't have a special power, some knowledge that would make someone want you back?"

"There's nothing special about me." Obie shook his head and thought about his time in Nefandus. His servitude had been endless, with no hope of relief—nothing unusual in that—but the way he had escaped had been odd. Master Hawkwick had left a forbidden book on the desk near the fireplace. Obie had found it and thumbed through the pages. Even through his drug-thickened haze, he knew that the simple leather-bound pages told him how to escape back to his own time.

Hawkwick had never been that careless before. With his mind now clear, Obie had a deep sense that Hawkwick had purposely left the book out for him to find. Maybe he had displeased Hawkwick, and he had hoped Obie would be brave enough to flee, but *servi* were never released from their bondage. At times they were destroyed, or sold to the hard-labor camps, but Obie had never heard of one gaining his freedom.

Now he wished he had brought the book with him, or at least read it completely before leaving. But *servi* were kept drugged, to keep them from thinking clearly, and at the time he had been too afraid Hawkwick would find him with it. He had been stupid to leave the book behind, but he had thought he'd return to his homeland, and Dominique had been eager to escape with him. Even now, if he concentrated on his drug-fogged memories, he was certain he had read that he could return to his own time. He let out a sigh, wondering why fate had trapped him here. What did destiny want with him?

"Hey, Obie!" Berto stepped into the kitchen, pulling a shopping bag from his backpack. His leather vest flapped open, revealing a strong, tight stomach and muscled chest. He wore his jeans low and the elastic band of his underwear peeked over the top of his waistband. He took a large paper crate with holes on the side and tossed it at Obie. "Catch!"

Obie caught it; something large squirmed inside. He dropped it, startled, and stepped back as a green lizard peered out at him. "What is it?"

"An iguana," Kyle said, returning to the kitchen and pinching the ends of his moussed hair into spikes.

"No, man," Berto said. "That's not an iguana, that's dinner. We're going to boil it, then roast it."

The iguana twitched and gazed at Obie. "I'm not letting you kill this guy." Obie bent over and took it from the box, surprised the iguana would let him hold it.

"You can't get attached to dinner," Berto teased and set more white cartons on the counter.

"Did you get takeout?" Kyle asked hungrily and opened a box. Grasshoppers jumped out and fled along the counter.

"You eat the things other people feed their pets," Obie joked.

"At least I don't eat my meat raw like a barbarian," Berto retorted, and he took out a cast-iron skillet. He set it on the stove and began roasting spices. A pungent aroma filled the kitchen.

Kyle glanced down at his watch. "Got to go." He headed out the back.

"Kyle always bails on us when it's time to eat." Berto grinned. "I don't know what he's got against the way we eat. You put a little garlic, lemon, and salt on the grasshoppers, and they're crunchier and better than any potato chip."

"Don't they jump out of your mouth?" Obie asked, not convinced.

"You don't eat 'em live." Berto laughed and went back to his cooking.

Obie stuffed another bite of hamburger into his mouth, then grabbed the carton of curdled milk and, ignoring the table and chairs, sat in the sunlight, sipping the sour liquid. He leaned back against the wall and watched Berto cook.

Berto's real name was Yaolt Ehecatl. It

meant "wind warrior." Obie admired the way Berto seemed to adjust so easily to this new world, but, like Obie, Berto also wanted to go home. He prayed to Tezcatlipoca, the lord of the smoking mirror and protector of slaves, hoping that the Toltec god would help him return to his own time.

Berto was a dream walker. In his sleep or a trance, he could journey to distant places. But while his spirit roamed, his body remained open and unguarded, easy for demons or lost spirits to possess. Berto had told Obie that a silver cord connected his soul to his body, but Obie wondered what would happen if someone severed the cord. How would Berto find his way back then?

"What time are you supposed to meet the band?" Berto asked, interrupting Obie's thoughts.

"Five-thirty," Obie answered.

"Man, you're late already," Berto said. "I'll give you a ride. Get your stuff."

Obie didn't move. "I've got an amp and my guitar."

"So what?" Berto left the room.

Obie hesitated. It wasn't just concern about his amp. Berto owned a Yamaha Road Star Warrior and Obie had seen him ride the bike. Obie glanced at the clock. He had only half an hour to get across town. Maybe he should call a cab. After this afternoon, he felt that changing to shadow was too risky. Still, he had to get there in time to try out the new amp with the speakers, and the band had to do a sound check.

He cursed silently in a language Berto wouldn't understand, then stood and went to his room. He put his guitar in a soft canvas case he could wear over his shoulder, then hoisted up his amp. His heart had already found a faster rate, just anticipating the wicked ride.

"What's wrong with you?" Berto's voice interrupted his thoughts. "Aren't you coming?" Berto stood in the hall, slipping into a leather jacket, his denim jeans torn at the knees.

"I don't have a helmet," Obie replied, looking for an excuse. He knew that a helmet was required by law.

Berto flashed him a toothy grin. "Neither do I."

Minutes later, Obie stood at the curb. Berto straddled the bike, turned the key, and opened the clutch. The engine snorted and growled.

Obie felt like turning to shadow right there, and catching a breeze across town.

"Climb on," Berto said. "It's safe."

"Yeah, right," Obie said, certain Berto couldn't hear him above the roar. Obie flung the guitar over his back, then muttered a prayer and, carefully balancing the amp, swung his leg over and straddled the bike.

Before he had even braced himself, Berto took off. Obie clenched the bike with his knees as Berto leaned to the right and took the corner at incredible speed. The engine bellowed, and its vibration shuddered through Obie. Air slapped around Berto and hit Obie's face, blowing back his hair.

Obie didn't know a lot about driving, but he knew there were speed limits and Berto was hanging it out, way past anything legal. He was about to yell something when the traffic stalled, then came to a stop.

But before Obie could relax, Berto leaned to the left and the bike split through the congested lanes. Idling cars and trucks spit exhaust into the air, making breathing difficult. Obie held on tightly, imagining a front fender sideswiping them and sending them crashing into a truck.

Berto carved through traffic, zipping the bike erratically back and forth, bobbing over the white plastic lane-dividing dots. The handlebar grazed the bumper of a Range Rover, but even that didn't slow Berto. He turned the throttle and increased the speed, rocketing through the slot between the cars.

Adrenaline fired through Obie, certain he was going to end up no more than a smear of blood and bone on the pavement.

CHAPTER FIVE

THE LIGHTS WENT OUT in the huge auditorium, and the audience became restless for Pagan to take the stage. Obie, Dacey, Nolo, and Les took their places behind the curtains. Then Nolo hit the drums and thunder rumbled through the auditorium, mimicking the noise the Visigoth warriors had made beating on their shields.

The audience screamed in anticipation as the curtains opened and the lights flashed. Kids pressed toward the stage.

Obie, Dacey and Les hummed into their microphones. Obie had written this piece, but it didn't belong to him. The *baritus* were the songs his people sang, to build their courage and terrify their enemies before going into battle. Obie remembered holding his shield in front of his face and yelling. The other warriors had done the same, until all their voices had swelled together, becoming fuller and deeper, and echoing to the sky. Now, in imitation, he, Dacey, and Les chanted.

At last Obie stepped back and worked his guitar, fingers cramped and straining to create the same tone the Visigoths had made. The new amp produced an unearthly bellow, bluesy and heavy. When he reached the crescendo, he and Dacey broke into a soaring vocal. Obie threw his head back and opened his mouth. He let out a wail, his battle cry, and the sound made him homesick for what he had once been. He closed his eyes, and, in his mind, he was rushing into battle, splashing over cold marshland.

His thoughts were shattered by someone calling his name. He looked out at the audience. It was impossible to hear one voice above the others, and yet he had clearly heard someone cry "Omer!" his given name.

Dacey glanced at him and moved closer,

strumming a quickening beat; the deep bass gave the song new energy.

Obie began to sing. His eyes swept over the audience and for the briefest moment he thought he saw Inna, the girl he had loved in his own time. He tried to catch a better look at the girl, but she was hidden now in a sea of bobbing heads.

Another girl, sitting on a guy's shoulders near the stage, caught his eye.

"Obie!" She ripped open her shirt and flashed her bra at him.

He smiled and she shimmied in response, but his smile wasn't for her. He was remembering a sweeter time, centuries before, when he had been in love with Inna. He stepped to the edge of the stage, searching again for the girl who had looked like her.

Girl-fans in the audience pressed forward, straining to touch him, stretching out their hands to grab his boots and the cuffs of his jeans. In his memory, Obie was falling far away, crossing time to the night he had first held Inna in his arms.

He had wanted to marry her and had offered her family a dowry for the honor; a yoked ox, a bridled horse, and a shield with spear and sword. That was before his father had banished her people from their tribe. King Filimer detested the Haliurunnae women, because they had engaged in magic with the world of the dead. But Obie had thought their rituals were no worse than the sacrifices and *dulths*, his father had ordered.

Inna might have been a sorceress, but he had never sensed anything evil about her. His father had insisted that she had entranced Obie with her mind-paralyzing skills and made it impossible for Obie to sense her wickedness. Obie wondered what had happened to her, and her people. Rumors had spread that the Haliurunnae women had entered into union with the evil spirits of the steppes and that had given them the power to come back and kill his father. The vindictiveness of the Haliurunnae was well known, and they had vowed to retaliate and destroy King Filimer and all his descendants.

Dacey let out a deep guttural howl that burst through Obie's reverie, and the opening song ended.

Time for your solo, Dacey mouthed.

Obie nervously stepped forward and glanced at the wires connected to his amp. He waited, counting the beat in his head. His right hand struck the first note. The tone hung in the air, and then he attacked, playing a machine-gun arpeggio. His fingers flew over the fret board, ending in a rich, harmonic slide.

The crowd went wild with applause and yells.

Then Nolo hit the drums, hammering the backbeat. Kids in the audience followed the rhythm, marking it with pounding heads and fists.

Obie rested his lips against the mike and sang, his lungs pushing out the primitive pain of having his world taken away. He closed his eyes. The drums picked up the beat, and then the base came in with a chugging locomotive rhythm.

When Obie played guitar, he forgot the

misery of being stranded in a world of concrete and automobile exhaust.

At last his spirit stepped into another, safer place; there was only Obie, his guitar and voice, everything else around him faded. Even the screaming spectators seemed far away. He didn't feel the evil spirit trying to pull him back to the past. Music was an anchor now, keeping him firmly attached to this world.

CHAPTER SIX

WHEN THE MUSIC ended, no one left the auditorium. A hundred kids stomped, clapped, whistled, and yelled, the noise rising into a deafening clamor. They wanted Pagan to stay on stage and play. Sweat dripped off Obie's forehead, running down his arms, neck, and chest. He wiped his face with the tail of his T-shirt.

"Obie!" Girls near the stage called out. "Throw us your shirt!"

Obie smiled, confused.

"Enjoy it, *hombre*!" Nolo whooped, then threw his sticks to the crowd and watched the kids fight to claim them.

Obie pulled a soft cloth from his back pocket and started wiping sweat off his guitar.

"What are you doing?" Dacey shouted and tossed his pick toward the outstretched hands. "We need to get out of here before pandemonium breaks loose."

Two girls fought their way past the line of security guards. They clambered onstage and threw themselves at Obie. He lost his balance and staggered back, laughing, but now he understood why the others wanted to leave.

Obie grabbed his jean jacket off the floor, then followed Les and Dacey outside. A stretch limo was parked near the back entrance, the motor idling for a fast getaway. The driver opened the rear door when he saw them.

"Where'd the car come from?" Obie asked, still a bit baffled.

"Me!" Dacey jumped into the back, threw himself across the rear-facing seat, and grabbed a soda from the ice bin. "Live fast, die young!" he raised the can, offering his toast, then popped the top and guzzled the Coke. He belched loudly and wiped his mouth. "Get in before the mob gets here."

"I've got other plans," Obie lied. He had none, but he knew the others usually spent almost all the money they earned from performing in the celebration afterward. They acted as if one show gave them endless cash, but Obie had lived through too much history not to know that fortunes changed rapidly.

"You're weird, dude." Nolo edged around Obie and slid into the car. He stretched his long, thin legs and pulled a California driver's license from his back jeans pocket. He flicked it with his finger. Obie's photo was on the front. "We got you a fake ID. And even if we hadn't, no one's going to hassle you tonight."

"Don't you want to go to the Whiskey?" Les asked. "Think of all those girls dying to meet you."

His choice of words triggered bad memories, and Obie's stomach clenched. His feral nature, the part of his character nurtured in Nefandus, felt strong tonight, and he didn't understand why. Maybe the power of the music had released his hidden and dark side. "Another time."

The other guys were easily eight to ten years older than Obie, and he'd heard enough about the seedy underground scene in Hollywood from them to know a night of partying could release the predator inside him.

Les hung one arm around Obie's neck, then shot his other hand high into the air, pinkie and index finger extended. "Rock and roll!" he shouted.

A group of girls had been lolling around the entrance to the parking lot. Now they turned, waved, and broke into a run, heading for the limo.

"C'mon, hurry up." Les grinned and dived inside.

"I'll catch you later." Obie hopped backward into the shadows. "Don't get too wiped out!" he yelled. "We've got the audition tomorrow, remember?"

The others waved him off. He could tell that they thought he was afraid. Fear was an element. He was terrified he'd lose control of that part of him that had enjoyed his nightmare existence in Nefandus.

The gleaming black car rolled away as girls knocked on the windows, slapped the fenders, and hit the bumpers, trying to get the driver to stop. One girl bravely jumped onto the hood, then slid off as the limo started to turn.

Obie used the distraction as a chance to break away. He eased into the shadows at the back of the parking lot, but a girl spied him.

"Obie!" she squealed. "Can we get your autograph?"

No one waited for an answer. Fifteen fans or more ran, giggling, waving, and shouting his name. His ability to monitor his dark side was weakening. He feared he wouldn't be able to keep it in check. What would happen when the girls swooped down on him?

Footsteps battered the ground behind him. He ducked around a corner, into a desolate backstreet that might have been a service entrance to a grocery store. He shook out his shoulders and forced his body to go slack, but the part of him that wanted to stay was growing stronger. Finally, his flesh unraveled into dark threads, and untied itself from gravity. He drifted into the cool damp. The night embraced him, a narrow streak of black, silky smoke. His vision was panoramic now, and each murky shade became distinct and isolated from the others, giving the nighttime shadows texture and dimension.

The girls turned the corner, stopped, and groaned with disappointment.

"Where'd he go?" a girl in graffiti-covered jeans asked.

Obie knew he should float away, but instead he circled the girls unseen, loving the fragrant mix of their perfumes and lotions. He lingered, even though it was wrong to stay. He felt free and uninhibited, at one with the night, a sensation he hadn't felt for a long time. He breezed around a girl with lush black hair, giving her a ghostly caress.

"What's that?" the girl asked. She rubbed her arms, then her knees.

Without warning, something foreign wove through Obie, as if another apparition were having some fun of its own. Suddenly pain burst through him like firecrackers shooting off. He fell to the ground, in solid form again, and knocked his head on concrete. Bright lights flashed behind his eyes, and he groaned. His arms and legs felt as if fire ants were swarming under his skin. He'd never materialized against his will before. What force had found him?

"Obie, what happened?" a girl with long earrings knelt beside him, and placed his head in her lap.

His eyes readjusted to the dark, the shifting shadows camouflaged by the night. Anything could be hiding from him now. He saw nothing above him to account for the strange sensation of colliding with something wraithlike.

The girls crowded closer, their beautiful eyes filled with concern, their heads forming a circle around him.

"He must have fallen off the balcony," one said.

"Do you want me to call an ambulance?" Another girl held her cell phone open in her hand, ready to call 911.

"I'm fine." He sat up and took long deep breaths, trying to calm himself.

Hands pressed toward his face, holding papers and pens, T-shirts, and the orange flyers for that night's show. He took a felt marker from the first girl and hurried through the signing.

Minutes later, the last girl kissed his forehead. "Thanks, Obie."

He stood, and leaned against a stack of crates. He felt breathless and edgy, and tried to relax his body so he could fade and float back to the apartment. He couldn't dissolve with his muscles tense and pumped with adrenaline.

From the corner of his eye he caught movement, and he stopped. A girl leaned against the stucco wall near him. He didn't recognize her at first. Then Kirsten stepped forward and walked carefully toward him, her shirt unbuttoned, revealing a halter top. A glitter design sparkled on her cheekbone.

"Hi, Obie," Kirsten said. "I was waiting for the others to leave so I could get your autograph." She pressed one silver-painted fingernail to her belly. "Sign me."

"Kirsten? Are you all right?" Obie felt uncomfortable and stepped away from her.

"Yes, silly. I just want your autograph." She let her hand stray and slide up his arm. Obviously, she wanted more than a signature.

"You don't want it," Obie whispered, feeling something old and ugly awaken inside him and begin to prowl. "I promise, not from me." He eased back again, hoping she would leave before it was too late. He was a danger to her. If he tried to kiss her, he'd absorb her life spirit. It was one more curse put upon the *servi*; they had been forced to feed on souls.

She bit her lip and followed him, then let her fingers trace over his belt buckle. "I really like you, Obie."

"It's my music you like, not me," he said, knowing time was running out. He took another step back and backed into a wall.

"I know what I want." She wrapped her hands around his waist and pressed herself tight against his body.

He closed his eyes and breathed in the sweet, jasmine fragrance of her hair.

"Why are you willing to sacrifice yourself for my music?" he asked softly, trying to understand. Among his people, one chose a single mate and no other; loyalty was everything. For both sexes, only virgins could marry.

"When you sing and play your guitar, it makes me feel things." Her hands slipped under his T-shirt, and fanned out over his chest. "Things I've never felt before."

"Music unlocks your soul," Obie whispered. "You're only feeling what's inside you."

"Then I must love you." She lifted her head for a kiss.

Evil awakened inside him, making his desire unbearable. Still, he tried to push it back, but he could feel the hunger becoming stronger than his ability to control it.

"Most guys would have kissed me by now," she said, interrupting his thoughts. Her hands pulled against his back, inviting him.

His lips hovered inches above hers. A short kiss couldn't hurt, could it? But what if he couldn't stop? Standing this close to her, feeling the softness of her body against his, the unholy part of him demanded release. Something was wrong. Normally he had more control over this impulse.

He lifted his arm and in the dim light glanced at the inscription he had written on his wrist for protection. With a shock, he realized that his perspiration had blurred the ink. His heart raced. No wonder he felt tempted. The runic letters had blended into a smudge. The writing was never meant to safeguard him from the threat of outside forces. He always inscribed the words in order to protect him from the evil hunger that lived and grew malignantly inside him. Now, he tried to mark *algiz*, for protection, to save himself from what he was about to do. His finger drew one line and stopped. Darkness took over, pulsing through him, free and powerful. He wanted her soul.

"Obie," Kirsten called impatiently, her breath sweet and tickling against his ear. "We can go back to my house. My parents aren't home."

"We can stay here," he whispered, and stole a glance at her to remember the life in her eyes. He kissed her and any resistance that remained inside him, fell away. The taste of her lipstick and the feel of her tongue aroused a need he hadn't felt since arriving in Los Angeles three months ago.

Her eyes opened, too late, as if she were having second thoughts. He kissed her, savoring the draw of her spirit from her body into his own.

"No witnesses," he whispered, with an edge of foreboding, repeating the instructions Hawkwick had given him so often.

His body leeched the energy from her, but now he didn't want to stop. He'd drain the soul that gave her life, and what would happen then? Would she die, or continue to exist, a walking corpse?

CHAPTER SEVEN

ABRUPTLY, THOUGHTS OF Inna burst into Obie's mind. He pushed Kirsten away, wrestling with his evil instincts. His hand came up and slashed the air, drawing *algiz*. The letter glowed, and its light impaled him, filling him with enough strength to fight for now. But he had to get away from Kirsten.

"Wait for love," he whispered, scooting sideways outside her reach. "It's worth the wait."

Kirsten blinked and gawked at him, confused, her eyes glassy with tears. "Did I faint? What happened?"

"Nothing happened," he reassured her.

She looked bewildered, but not helpless. She buttoned her shirt as if suddenly cold.

He backed away. This time she let him go. He lingered only long enough to watch her reach the safety of the club. Then he started running, his boots pounding down the middle of the deserted street, the exercise releasing pent-up emotion. What was he going to do now? Kyle had warned him to be more careful. Maybe his only solution was to leave L.A. The border between the two worlds seemed thinner here. He'd been thinking about going anyway.

He changed direction and sprinted into an alley, preferring darkness and shadow to the garish neon lights and the glare from streetlamps. He found his stride, and the world around him fell away. The sound of his own breathing filled the silence and he imagined he was running through a black-night forest, his footprints the only ones for miles. His boot hit a pothole, and he pretended it was a craggy root. Happiness surged through him, remembering his life, the way the evergreens had filled his lungs with their aromatic scent of pine resin. Tears came to his eyes.

An hour later Obie reached Chinatown and slowed his pace, his mouth dry, his muscles fatigued. Shop owners swept the sidewalks in front of their stores and cleaned their front windows, preparing for the next day. The smells of ammonia and detergent floated into the air.

Obie picked up a running hose and drank from the nozzle. He was still drinking when he was stricken with the feeling that an enemy was crouching near. He threw the hose aside and hid in a passageway between two stores, near a line of black plastic trash bags. He saw nothing unusual. But the skills his father had taught him long ago came into play. He sensed someone near, watching him, and he didn't think it was a fan. A fan would have shown herself by now. Even a *venator* wouldn't have waited this long to attack. That left Sledge, Forrest, and Barry. Could Barry have convinced the other two that there was something supernaturally different about Obie? Maybe those three were hanging back, clumsily following him to see if he would do something strange and prove Barry's suspicions correct.

Obie stepped around the piled trash bags, setting a trap of his own. He continued down the narrow passageway, taking slow, easy steps so that whoever hunted him wouldn't think he was getting away. His boots splashed through puddles and when he heard a scuffling sound behind him, he whirled around.

Shadows billowed, reshaping, and fell flat against the wall. Had the movement only been a trick of the eye or had he caught something? He stepped closer, and stared at the blackened bricks. The charred look could have come from a past fire. Or maybe a shape-shifter was clinging to the building. He ran his hand over the cold wall, but he felt no vibration or hidden life in the rough and soot-covered bricks.

He looked both ways, but each time an empty passage stared back at him. Still, the sense of its being haunted didn't go away. He waited, with the patience of a predator, crouched and tense, but no shift of stance, or whisper gave anyone away.

Suddenly a dog yelped in an open window overhead, startling him. A different dog began to howl, and then another barked, until every dog in the neighborhood was growling and yelping. Soon, impatient voices joined the baying, people yelling at the animals to be quiet, but the barking continued, as if the animals had sensed the same disturbance that enveloped Obie.

He still didn't see anything but on some primitive level he clearly sensed the danger. His heart raced and a cold sweat prickled his forehead, then beneath the dog chorus came a new sound, a scuttling that made Obie look down. Fear crept up his spine. A runic inscription swept toward him, the letters interlocked in a chain. Only a powerful sorcerer could send a spell like the one racing toward him. He inched back but didn't run. He needed to read the letters but when he did he felt worse. The spell was one cast to capture him. He knew he should leave but he remained, hoping to find a clue to tell him who had sent the magic.

Abruptly the words changed direction and slipped into a puddle. The water bubbled, then turned to steam, as if whoever had sent the charm, had suddenly become aware that Obie had seen it. But who could be the force behind the inscription?

Master Hawkwick knew nothing about rune magic, and the women of the Haliurunnae clan had died out a thousand years ago. But then, he had survived in Nefandus, so why couldn't the Haliurunnae have also found a safe haven in this world, or another? Was it possible his sworn enemies still lived?

He continued toward the apartment, the feel of magic growing stronger, until he could taste the inimitable flavor of a strong spell.

Near the entrance to his apartment, a girl stood in the shadows, her back to Obie, her face lifted to the moon. She stepped into the dark and turned, her attention fixed on him. She was dressed oddly in a long cloak trimmed with fur and fastened with a gold brooch that caught the streetlight.

"Omer," she whispered.

He hadn't heard anyone speak his real name since leaving Nefandus. Was she a *vena-*

trix? He'd never had an encounter with a female bounty hunter before. Her hands were empty, but she could have had a weapon hidden beneath her cloak. He stopped and broke into a sudden sweat.

CHAPTER EIGHT

"WHY ARE YOU AFRAID of me?" The girl whispered, and glided silently into the light, her hair as white as moonglow.

"Inna?" Obie blinked, certain she was only a projection of his imagination created by his intense loneliness.

"It's really me," she said, and drifted closer, her body buoyed by air. Soft ringlets framed her face and curled down to her waist.

"How did you cross time to see me?" he said with wonder, his mind already racing to other possibilities; maybe he could go home with her.

But then she held up her arm, beautifully muscled, and he saw the runic inscription on her gold bracelet. Cold fear spread through him. His concern wasn't for himself, but for Inna. She was a spirit messenger. Someone had awakened her sleeping soul with magic and sent her to him. She existed only for as long as the sorcerer needed her, and then, unless someone freed her, she would drift aimlessly, without rest, easily summoned by others with evil intent.

"Who's done this to you?" he asked, determined to free her. "I don't remember my runes, but you can tell me what to do to release you from the binding."

She jangled the bracelet. "I sent myself forth to find you."

"Then why didn't you come before now?" he said, hating the accusatory tone that had slipped into his voice.

"I couldn't find you. Do you think it has been easy, crossing so many years? I never would have found you if someone more powerful hadn't invoked a spell that left a trail for me to follow. I'm not the only one who has been trying to locate you. Why has the air become filled with incantations to capture you?"

Obie shook his head, wondering if she was telling him the truth. "I don't know."

"Come with me." She held out her hand, and the inscription on her bracelet grew brighter, as if some new and potent magic were working.

"Are you taking me home?" he asked, trying to push back the hope stirring inside him.

"I'm sorry," she whispered sadly. "I don't have that kind of power."

"You did once," he argued.

"Your destiny lies here, in this time," she answered. "No one may defy fate, but if you come with me now, we can be safe for a few moments before I have to return, and then I can tell you what I know."

"Tell me here," he said.

Her head turned, and she gazed at the shadows behind her, as if suddenly aware of something disturbing her incantation.

"Hurry," she said and offered her hand. "I have to leave."

He stared at her, undecided. Could he trust her enough to let the strong magic circling her bind him? Inna was one of the Haliurunnae. Her people had brutally murdered his father and had sworn to destroy all the descendants of King Filimer.

"Did you send an inscription a few minutes ago to trap me?" he asked, wondering if she would admit the truth if she had.

"No, I've come only to warn you," she said, impatiently.

Now he felt something drawing at the air, like a magic lodestone overpowering her spell and draining it. The shimmer behind her began to dull.

"Someone else is trying to capture you," she said, "and is coming quickly. Please." She held out her hand again, impatiently wiggling her fingers. "I have much I need to tell you."

"Who's coming?" he asked, stepping away from her, his mind muddled, not sure yet if he could trust her. "If it's true what you say, then tell me a name."

"I can't believe you've lost your daring," she said as a breeze began to whirl around her. Her cloak flapped wildly. "There was a time when you were brave, but I see you've let your hair grow long again."

He didn't rise to her challenge. All Visigoth boys, when they reached a certain age, let their hair grow long and didn't cut it again until after they had killed an enemy in battle. He had earned the right to cut his hair, but he kept it long now in shame, and did not intend to cut it again until he had avenged his father's death.

"I had thought you would be happy to see me," she said, her voice fading in the fierce wind.

Sadness overcame him. He looked into her deep, blue eyes and could feel her thoughts cross his mind, searching for the love he had once felt for her. Her mental grip tightened, and he wondered why she was trying to entrance him, but since their last encounter he had developed strength of his own. He resisted; her eyes widened with surprise.

"What have you become?" she asked. Her hair twirled about her face, rising sinuously around her, caught in a gust, and she held onto his arm as if she were struggling to stay.

Did she think he had become a sorcerer, a necromancer or something more? "I lived in Nefandus," he answered at last.

She recoiled as if he were something foul and unclean. Her cloak swirled around her, coiling tightly, and she vanished, leaving a trail of sparkling mist and the strong scent of magic.

Even though she was gone, her whisper tickled across his cheek. "If you won't go with me, you must at least believe me, or all with be lost."

"Believe what?" he asked the night air.

Inna's disembodied voice came again. "The Haliurunnae did not kill your father."

But before she could say more, a furious whirlwind swept around him, as if whatever magic had been following Inna were trying to stop her from saying more. As quickly as the wind had come, it died, and silence returned.

Obie stood alone and pinched the bridge of his nose against the gathering tears. With dread, he looked back to where Inna had stood when he had first come down the street. What evil sorcerer had awakened her and now controlled her spirit? Or had she told him the truth—could she really have journeyed so far across time?

Then a small gray stone dropped from the air, pinged against the concrete, and bounced into a scattering of weeds. Obie picked it up and felt its power vibrate against his palm. The Hellerune was cut into its surface and stained with blood. Each character of the runic alphabet had its own magical power or caused the release of magic simply by being cut or named. This runic symbol could unleash the mysteries of death and hell. The Haliurunnae used it to conjure the dead. Why would Inna give him such a powerful stone if she was his enemy?

His stomach cramped as he realized what his question implied. If the rune was real, then that meant Inna had told the truth. She had come to help him, and he hadn't trusted her. Regret besieged him. He should have gone with her.

CHAPTER NINE

OBIE STARTED TOWARD the apartment, his spirits low. A heavy and dismal mood had descended upon him. He didn't want to go inside. Light glowed from the top floor, and he could see Kyle working at one of the long tables near his easel. Obie didn't know what he would do if Kyle started questioning him again. In his sinking mood, he might tell Kyle about Inna's visit, and somehow Obie felt it was better to keep that meeting secret for now.

He spread his arms, embracing the night, and let his body foam out. His silhouette rose, surrendering to a moist, ocean breeze, and he drifted higher and higher, until his windswept form became an inky spiral.

The air seemed to soften above the city, away from concrete and brick, but the heartsick feeling didn't leave him. Regret burdened him with a joylessness he hadn't felt since his first days in Nefandus, when he had faced an endless life as a *servus*. His aunt had lured him there with promises of a better and safer life. He had thought she was trying to protect him, but soon realized she had wanted to use him to find his mother's runes. When he hadn't cooperated, she had given him to Hawkwick.

Now, as he bobbed through the gauzy clouds into the full moon's radiance, the lunar glow burned through him with purifying power, and brought back memories of late nights spent listening to his mother. She had been a rune master, her skills renowned. Everyone had respected and loved her. She had had the power to work miracles, and had tried to teach Obie to do the same, but he hadn't paid attention, and had never practiced with his runes. He hadn't understood then that each small choice he made was building his future. Now he wished he had been a better student, because if Inna had traveled to the present on magic, then, with the right incantation, he could journey back.

Abruptly, Obie felt a dangerous drop in his temperature and knew he had to become solid soon. Other shape-shifters seemed to regulate their vaporous bodies better, but this was just one more lesson he had failed to learn. He let his feet materialize. His heavy boots created drag, slowing his flight, and gently he drifted toward the ground, a blotch of black fog connected to two large feet.

He settled on Durand Drive in the hills above Los Angeles, and remolded himself into a hazy silhouette before he materialized. The salty taste of ocean air filled his mouth, and his hair and clothes were damp from his time in the thinning clouds. He took a tentative step and then another up a thorny hiking trail leading to the Hollywood sign. There were better views of the city from Sunset Boulevard, but Obie liked the forty-five-foot-high letters made of sheet-metal and painted white.

He wasn't the only one drawn here. In spite of the gated fence and hi-tech security cameras, homeless people camped on the slope. Three kids with dreams were lighting candles, as if this symbol of the movie industry could grant their wishes or, at least, give them a good part.

Motion detectors had been placed around the giant letters, but instead of keeping vandals away, they had helped make the sign a mecca for taggers. Two boys in long T-shirts and baggy shorts, hid spray cans and studied the letters, hoping to leave with boasting rights.

Obie climbed through sage scrub and prickly-pear cactus to a quiet spot above the sign. He sat down and stared out at the glittering city. Spotlights strafed the misty sky, and the moon peered through the withering clouds and left a glowing mark on Obie's skin, reminding him of what he had once been. He eased back into the shadows, and the long, lance-shaped leaves of California holly tickled his hair. Kyle had told him that Hollywood was named for the shrub.

Behind him the dry brush crackled with the

distinctive sound of stealthy footsteps. The chaparral was thick and able to hide someone sneaking up on him. His hands went cold, and he crouched, ready to spring.

A twig snapped, and then another.

He relaxed his arms and started to fade, but before he could turn to shadow, someone nudged his evaporating body with a toe. He reassembled with a jolt and turned.

Berto stood behind him, grinning. In one hand, he dangled four beer cans from their plastic holder, and in the other he held an open can. "I didn't expect to see you."

"Bad night," Obie said, and settled back again. "I thought you were a bounty hunter sneaking up on me."

Berto accepted the explanation and sat down. "Why are you up here?"

Obie picked up a pebble and threw it. How could he tell Berto what was really troubling him? He'd let his one chance to tell Inna how much he loved her slip away. Now he feared she would remember him as someone obscene and defiled who had lived in Nefandus.

"Things are getting complicated," Obie said. "Why are you here?"

"Kyle's been weirding out on me with the way he's afraid I'm attracting bounty hunters," Berto said.

"You, too?" Obie asked, suddenly feeling more comfortable knowing he wasn't the only one Kyle suspected of putting them in danger.

Berto nodded. "Kyle attracts them on his own. He hasn't figured that out yet. Or maybe it's just easier for him to blame you and me. He's got too many secrets and sometimes I think he really does forget that he's a Renegade, too."

"Have you talked to him about it?" Obie asked.

"Only about a dozen times," Berto said. "The last time the argument ended in a brawl. Kyle knows it's the truth, or he wouldn't be so defensive."

"The truth is hard," Obie said, remembering the look of disgust on Inna's face. "Do you think our existence is a sin? I mean, everything is supposed to die. You agree to life, knowing it has to end, and we—"

"Go on forever," Berto said.

"But I'm afraid to get back in the cycle of living and dying," Obie said. "I'm scared because of what I've done. Do you think we're responsible if someone else made us do those things?"

"Yes," Berto said, and swigged his beer.

Obie looked at Berto in the moon's light, wondering if their lives in Nefandus had been the same. Berto seemed indifferent to the moon's glow, but Obie craved it, because its light seemed to cleanse him.

"Maybe our existence is wrong," Berto said at last. "But I don't know any way to change it except to go back in time and live out a life the way it was always meant to be."

"What do you think happens to us if we can't find a way to return to our own time?" Obie said quietly.

"Our friends will start aging," Berto said. "But we won't."

"I've got to find a friend first," Obie said, trying to lighten the mood.

"We'll have to move to some other city

eventually," Berto said. "And I guess Kyle will make us enroll in another high school and then another."

"I'll go back to Nefandus before I'll spend an eternity in high school." Obie would remain fifteen forever, but he was glad he had his teenage strength and height at least. Some *servi* stayed children forever. "Maybe it's best to just run away now," Obie said quietly.

"Running doesn't work," Berto said and leaned back on his arms. "I tried. I went down to Mexico to the old Toltec kingdom of Tula,"

"That's where you went when you disappeared?" Obie asked.

Berto nodded. "I went to the Templo de Tlahuizcalpantecuhtli," Berto said softly. "You have to have the courage to face and know yourself to go there. It was the center of spiritual knowledge. I went there to transcend."

"You mean, to escape what we are?" Obie asked.

Berto nodded. "I sat on the pyramid and shifted the source of my personal power from my mind to my spirit. I let the silent knowledge that's always around us come into me to create the energy I needed, and then I fell into a dream."

Obie waited for Berto to go on.

"A guide came—" Berto said reverently.

"Who?" Obie asked impatiently.

"Tezcatlipoca." Berto stared at Obie. "In the dream, the great lord brought me back here. I had traveled down by bus and foot to the temple in Mexico, but when I woke up I was sitting back in our loft apartment again, as if I'd never left. My destiny is here. There's a reason we've come together here in this time."

"Sometimes fate guides us," Obie said repeating his mother's words.

Obie remembered his mother late at night spilling the small gray rune stones from her charm pouch onto the pelts covering his bed. Each time the blank rune had dominated her cast. He had been too young then to understand how unusual that was. She could do nothing to change his fate and had cautioned him to accept his future with stoic bravery. But when he had asked if bad fortune waited for him, she had told him that no destiny was bad because all were decreed by the divine.

Now he wondered what she had seen.

CHAPTER TEN

OBIE SCREAMED HIMSELF awake, but the night terror didn't release him, and in his dream world, he frantically pressed his hands into the blood surging from his father's wound. The nightmare faded, and Obie opened his eyes, disoriented. He shook his head and let the confusion drop away. He was kneeling, his hands pressed in the gravelly dirt. The last beer had spilled and was frothing warmly over his fingers. He breathed the familiar fermented smell and licked the tears on his lips, then wiped his hands down his jeans and sat back.

A homeless woman in the bushes watched him with wary eyes from beneath a sheet of blue plastic. His yelling had awakened her, but Berto had slept on; he had lived in Nefandus, and screams of rage, pain, and terror were there like the background of traffic sounds in L.A.

Obie gulped the morning air, trying to soothe his heart. The day his father had died, the winds had carried an odd song, warning of something bad, and that evening Obie had found his father in the forest, a sword sunk deep in his chest. Runic inscriptions had streamed ceaselessly over the hilt and blade, and his father's blood had stained the pale pine needles brown-red. The smell of dark magic had overpowered the natural scents of moss and evergreens. As in the dream, Obie had tried to stop the bleeding, but the flow had ended only when the death-giving goddess had taken his father.

Now the sun cut an orange slit across the gray horizon, and to the west a lazy fog bank lay on the ocean. Sparrows chattered overhead, and Obie's mouth tasted sour from sleep. He wanted to go back to the loft and get something to eat.

He stood and nudged Berto with the toe of his boot. "Come on. It's time."

Berto turned over, as if he didn't want to leave his dreams.

"We got to get back. I need some real sleep," Obie said and realized in that moment he had made a decision to stay in L.A. and not run away. The band had a live audition at Quake tonight so the owner could see how kids reacted to their playing, but Obie sensed it was only a way to get a night of free music.

Berto stretched, and then they trudged down the hillside in silence. On the street, Berto swung his leg over his bike. He stood, straddling the seat, and hit the kickstand with the back of his shoe. It sprang up. While Berto rocked the bike back and forth to make sure it was in neutral, Obie climbed on. The engine made a grinding sound and fired, and they zipped away.

The early morning streets were empty, except for an occasional bus or delivery truck, and without cars posing a threat, Obie understood why Berto loved the ride. They stopped at

Cantor's and bought breakfast to take home, and a few minutes later they walked through the door of their loft. The aroma of onions, potatoes, lox, and coffee came from the grease-stained bags they carried. Obie stepped into the large foyer and almost tripped over a pair of women's spike-heeled shoes.

"Kyle's got company," Berto said and hung his key on a hook. "That's good. At least he won't be questioning us about where we've been."

Obie followed Berto into the large room where Kyle had set up his art studio, and stopped. White high-heeled shoes in every size lay scattered over the drop cloths.

"How many girls has he got here?" Obie asked. "I didn't even know he had a girlfriend."

"We chose the wrong night to ditch him," Berto said, staring down at the shoes. "That's for sure."

"Hey!" Kyle jumped up, startling them both. He had been sleeping in the beanbag chair, hidden behind a table in the corner. Now he hurried to them, flipping the pages in a sketch pad, anxious to show them his drawing. "Look at this."

Obie stared dumbly at an illustration of a shoe, and then he glanced up at the silly smile on Kyle's face. Maybe the pressure of running from bounty hunters had finally gotten to Kyle.

"What about it?" Berto asked carefully.

"You know how guys customize their cars with paintings of the sea or women?" He turned the pages and showed different designs to paint on shoes; seascapes, floral sprays, and even a patriotic motif of red, white, and blue. "I sold four pairs of shoes to the actresses on the set last night, and Wardrobe ordered more. A dozen! They're going to use my shoes in the movie. I could start a trend."

"I like the look," Obie said, glad Kyle was preoccupied with something other than their absence overnight.

"Way past cool," Berto put in and picked up a pair of shoes drying on the table. A dragon's mouth covered the toe, and the scaly green body curled back to the heel. "What are you going to do with all the money?"

"Pay the gas bill, then take acting lessons," Kyle said, staring down at a drawing of a leopard. "Everything will be perfect if you guys will stay out of trouble."

Obie and Berto exchanged a secret look.

That afternoon Berto and Kyle went out, leaving Obie alone. Hours later, when they hadn't come home, Obie decided to get ready for the night's performance. The iguana followed him into the bathroom and scurried onto the counter, sunning under the light from the heat lamps in the ceiling. Obie turned the spigot in the shower stall. Steam rose and clouded the mirrors as he undressed. He started to step in, but as his toes touched the spray, he felt someone staring at him. He turned. Kyle and Berto stood at the bathroom door, peering in.

"What?" he asked, and grabbed a towel. The sudden movement startled the iguana and it scooted back.

"We decided its time for you to join the

modern world," Berto said. He walked across the tiled floor, stuck his hand into the shower stall and turned off the water.

"You're a rock star now," Kyle said, following Berto into the bathroom. He opened a black trash bag and gingerly picked up Obie's clothes and tossed them in. "You can't wear these hillbilly boots anymore, and that dirty jean jacket has got to go. Where'd you get your clothes, anyway?"

Obie shrugged and tucked the towel around his waist. He'd taken the clothes from a Salvation Army collection box when he'd first arrived, although he hadn't known at the time that he was stealing from a charity. "I like the jean jacket," Obie said, wondering what he'd wear on stage that night.

"You can't put on the same clothes every day," Berto added.

"Not unless you wash them at least once a week," Kyle agreed. "You're starting to stink."

"And what is it you don't understand about shaving?" Berto asked. "You got shag all over your face."

"We'll show you how," Kyle said, and took a plastic razor from the medicine cabinet.

"I know how," Obie said, wondering what was wrong with the way he looked.

"And you got to comb that hair." Berto grabbed a brush and scissors. "At least once a century."

Moments later, Obie stood under the glaring lights, freshly shaven. His hair was trimmed and washed, but still hung below his shoulders. Water dripped down his back, and the steamy air smelled of eucalyptus, spicy aftershave, and astringent.

Berto stole a glance at his watch. "We've got to hurry. We still have to get rid of the hair between your eyebrows and pierce your ear."

Minutes later, Obie stared into the mirror. His earlobe throbbed where Berto had tacked the silver stud. He definitely looked different, but he wasn't sure if he liked the new look or not.

"You look too Cali now," Kyle said, shaking his head. "I think we made a mistake."

"You're right," Berto added. "We went too far. I liked him better before."

Obie could feel his anger boiling over, but before it burst out in the new curse words he was learning, Berto smiled and started laughing. "But now you've had your initiation."

"Welcome to our tribe," Kyle said and clasped Obie's hand in a hearty handshake.

Then Berto dashed from the room and came back carrying shopping bags from Abercrombie and Old Navy. "We got you some clothes, kind of our way of saying you've arrived."

Obie glanced inside and smiled. He suddenly felt as if he belonged. "Thanks."

CHAPTER ELEVEN

NO SIGNS ADVERTISED Quake. During the day the large, windowless building looked abandoned, but at night kids in trendy clothes started gathering at the huge, carved door. Obie and Kyle cut across a nearby vacant lot. Stretch limousines were parked there and looked out of place next to tall weeds and cast-off oil drums. Across the street, valets in red vests guarded new Porsches and Ferraris.

The line curled down the block, three and four kids deep, but of the two hundred or more partygoers waiting to go in, fewer than half would be allowed to enter. Obie and Kyle headed for the entrance. The cool night breeze flowed around them, scented with perfume, aftershave, breath mints, and alcohol. A muffled *thump, thump, thump* came from the techno music inside.

Berto stood at the door, behind a burgundy velvet rope that was suspended between chrome poles set on pedestals. He held a clipboard in his hand, and a small plastic headset curled over his ear connecting him to security guards and valets. Girls flashed him eager smiles, hoping to get beyond the gate.

"Man, look at the crowd," Kyle said when they joined Berto.

"The owner hired some big mix-master to be the DJ tonight," Berto said, "but I think kids are mostly here hoping to hear Pagan play."

"Thanks," Obie said and peered over Berto's shoulder. "How many names are on the list?"

"The clipboard's just for show." Berto gave him a conspiring wink. "I'm not going to let just anyone in, even if there is room. They have to make the grade."

A guy with sleeve tattoos and a shaved head walked toward them. His strong cologne burned the air with its sharp and pungent smell. "Hey, Berto, how does it look for getting in tonight?"

"Great," Berto answered and scribbled *ass-hole* on the paper clipped to his board. "I got your name. Ralph, right?"

"That's right." The guy seemed pleased that Berto had remembered.

"I'd let you in right now," Berto continued, "if it weren't for the fire marshal, but your chances look good tonight." Berto wrote *never* and underlined it twice. "I'll let you know when there's room. I only have a few names in front of yours."

"Thanks." Ralph strolled back toward the end of the line, but stopped to talk to two girls with smoky eyes and rhinestone attitudes.

"Man, some day some bruiser is going to catch what you're doing," Kyle said, "and knock your teeth in."

"It'll never happen," Berto answered with confidence. "I give everyone hope. Besides, no one's ever disappointed; half the party is out here."

"Maybe the better half," Obie agreed. The atmosphere surged with energy.

A burly guy wearing platinum chains and diamond charms, walked up to the rope and slipped a hundred-dollar bill into Berto's pocket. "Berto, my man, is there any room left inside?"

"I've been holding your reservation." Berto unsnapped the silver hook, and held the velvet rope aside.

The guy nodded his thanks and pushed against the massive door. The sounds of techno music and laughter spilled outside. Two security guards in yellow jackets greeted him and he lifted his arms, familiar with their routine. The door closed, and the music again became to the barely audible *thump, thump, thump*.

"So is money how you determine if someone makes the grade?" Obie teased, and pulled at Berto's pocket to see how much he had collected.

"No," Berto said. "I'm completely unreliable." He ran a hand over his raven-black hair, now combed back tight in a ponytail. "That's what keeps the crowd coming back. They never know when I'm going to slip up and let them in. That's part of the game."

"Look who just arrived," Kyle said and nudged Obie.

An SUV pulled up to the curb across the street and parked illegally next to the fire hydrant. Sledge and Allison climbed out and hurried across the street, dodging between cars. Allison wore a slinky top and a low-slung mini, her legs long in spikey heels, her skin covered with a silky gloss. Sledge's huge hand rested on her bare hip. Anger rose in Obie, unexpected; he didn't like Sledge touching Allison, and he didn't understand why.

Allison wore a camera on a woven strap around her neck. When she reached the curb, she looked through the viewfinder, aimed at Obie and focused the lens. The flash went off.

Obie blinked, trying to clear his vision of the after-images from the glaring light.

Sledge sauntered over to Berto, obviously expecting to be let in. "Do you have room for us?" The mint in his mouth didn't mask his sour, beer breath. He pulled Allison in front of him and intimately rested his hands on her bare midriff.

"I can't let you in," Berto said.

"Why not?" Sledge asked, obviously surprised and displeased. He tried to steal a look at the papers on the clipboard.

"I'll add your name to my list," Berto said with authority.

"No one's going to know," Sledge coaxed. "We'll just slip in."

"I'm at maximum capacity." Berto frowned. "You're not getting in, so just deal with it like everyone else."

Obie glanced at Allison, wondering why she hung out with Sledge. He caught her eye, but she looked away.

"Maybe later," Sledge agreed with an insolent scowl, and then he whispered something to Allison. She nodded, and he wandered down the line, as if he were looking for someone.

As soon as Sledge left, Allison ducked under the rope before Berto could stop her. She eased next to Obie. The lens of her camera was pointed at him, but he put his hand up before she took the shot. He didn't want to be blinded by the flash again.

"Where's your friend off to?" Obie said, not bothering to hide his contempt.

"He's trying to find Forrest and Barry," she answered, and then, ignoring Obie's anger, she continued, "I'm sorry I accused you of borrowing money from my mom the other day. She explained everything to me. It's just that so many guys have used her and never paid her back. Sometimes it makes it hard."

Obie glanced down at her clearly expensive clothes and for some reason it irked him. "Why are you apologizing? You're already the queen of popularity. You don't need my vote."

Slick, Berto mouthed behind Allison. Kyle's eyes widened.

"I was just telling you I was wrong," Allison said, and her eyebrows folded into a peevish glare. "Most people are a little more gracious when someone apologizes."

"Go back to Sledge," Obie said rudely. He

hated the heavy, gut-wrenching sensation that told him he was being offensive, but his words seemed to have more power than his ability to hold them back. "Take a picture of him."

Allison huffed and said something under her breath. She stepped back, held up the camera and looked through the viewfinder. The shutter clicked, and the white flash made red and gray dots appear in front of Obie's vision again. Then, as if she had gotten what she had come for, she dodged under the rope and hurried away, her stiletto heels clicking.

"What's that bit with the camera?" Berto said, watching Allison. "Why is she taking pictures of you?"

"Obie's a star," Kyle said good-naturedly. "Maybe Allison is just another groupie."

"I don't like it," Berto said, seeming annoyed. "I get a bad feeling from her. She's hiding something." But before he could explain, his attention was taken up by five men in black suits, hurrying to the gate, conspicuously protecting a short, blond girl.

"Don't stare," Berto ordered in a hushed

voice and unhooked the rope. He opened the door, and the music grew loud again.

The first man slipped Berto a wad of bills, and, when he did, Obie caught a clear view of the girl they were escorting. Her long hair, perfect body, and big smile made it impossible not to recognize her. Her face graced the billboards on Sunset Boulevard.

"Get your tongue back in your mouth." Kyle elbowed him. "Berto told you not to stare. She has a thing about people looking at her."

"Why does she have so many bodyguards?" Obie watched the entourage go inside.

"Because nobody likes her," Berto explained. "The first time she was here, she got in a fight. She called the wrong girl a poser. Now she comes here with an army for protection."

Kyle motioned with his chin. "You got a bigger problem, Berto. Some of your rejects just slid inside. You'd better add them to your count."

Berto turned.

Sledge, Barry, Forrest, and Allison had

pushed inside while the door was open for the actress and her bodyguards.

But Berto didn't seem upset. He smiled good-naturedly. "Like I said, I give everybody hope. It keeps the crowd coming. They'll go back to school and tell everyone about their success, and that will make more kids want to come and try to get inside. I'm a customer magnet. My skills draw business."

"We'd better go in." Kyle pointed to his watch and opened the door. "It's almost time for Obie to play."

Obie started in, but paused, distracted by a sudden whiff of rose petals. The air was thick with various perfumes, but he had definitely caught a trace of magic.

"What is it?" Berto asked, suddenly searching the shadows.

"Magic," Obie said. "I thought I smelled it."

Kyle laughed. "Magic doesn't have any kind of smell."

Obie ignored him and took a deep breath, trying to catch the sweet smoky aroma again. "Strong magic has the scent of burning roses."

"Come on," Kyle said, pulling him toward the door. Obie stared out at the night. Finally he turned and followed Kyle inside. He held out his arms as a security guard passed a handheld metal detector over his legs. After an intense inspection, Obie continued in to the large, open room.

Music vibrated from mammoth speakers. Strobe lights flickered, giving the dancers the bizarre staccato look of flailing arms and haunted faces. Laser lights pulsed and the chrome decorations on the walls and ceilings reflected their sizzling colors. A long balcony looked down on the floor and more kids danced up there in silhouette. Berto had told him it was a VIP section where celebrities partied.

Then, over the bouncing heads and waving arms, Obie saw the other band members setting up on a small stage. He pressed through the crowd. Kyle was already dancing with a girl wearing pink gloves and a tiara of downy feathers. Her thick, black bangs hung into her eyes.

In the middle of the floor, Allison moved sinuously against Sledge, her back pressed against him, his hands on her hips pulling her closer. Envy made Obie's stomach clench and he suddenly wished he had accepted Allison's apology. He stared, nettled by bitter emotions, but there was nothing he could do.

CHAPTER TWELVE

PAGAN HAD BEEN PERFORMING for over an hour. Sweat dripped down Obie's back, and his hair clung to his neck. His chest prickled, itched and stung, but, worse, the jealous feeling hadn't gone away.

At the end of the next set, Dacey walked over to Obie and Les. He lifted his sunglasses. His eyes were bloodshot. "We rocked the house," Dacey said. "The owner has got to hire us after all this free play."

Obie nodded. "I think we've done enough."

"One last song," Les said hoarsely. "But no more. We're not working for charity."

Dacey grabbed the mike and thanked the audience. "It's been a joy playing for you, and now our time has come to 'An End.'"

Nolo started marking out the beat on the rim of his drum.

Obie's fingers ran across the frets, playing the introduction to their song, "An End." He scanned the audience. Allison was nestled under Sledge's arm now but she was not dancing. When Sledge caught her looking at Obie, he turned her chin with the tip of his finger and kissed her. Afterward he gazed back at Obie with an unreadable smile. Did he know Obie was having a crippling attack of jealousy?

The song finished and Obie felt an adrenaline rush. The crowd went wild. Kids whistled and clapped. In gratitude, he continued playing, throwing out explosive new tones in an E minor scale. The basic melody was something he'd written long ago and it matched his current mixed-up mood.

The house lights went on, and the DJ began setting up. Obie stopped his impromptu riff as techno music blasted from the giant speakers. Kids yelled, obviously excited and moved by what he'd played.

The DJ changed his music, then started scratching records. But he did it only long enough to get the crowd's attention away from Obie. After that he put on something Obie had heard on the radio at least fifty times. Everyone started dancing again, and under the house-lights, Obie could clearly see Sledge and Allison huddled close together, her camera dangling around her neck.

Dacey walked over to Obie. "I'm not kidding you," he said, taking off his sunglasses. "We were lucky the day our old lead guitar player ditched us to join a name band, because now we have you."

"Lucky for me," Obie said, remembering the flyer he'd seen taped on the lamppost, announcing auditions for guitar players.

"Write down the song you just played," Les said. "It was incredible. Even if it was for some girl."

"Girl?" Obie's head shot up.

"The one in the audience who kept taking

your picture," Les went on. "The camera flash was more annoying than the strobe lights. She moved from one side of the stage to the other trying to catch you."

"She did?" Obie had seen flashes, but all he's really noticed was Allison dancing with Sledge.

"That riff was mind-bending," Dacey said, pulling Obie's attention back to the music. "Where did you learn that stuff, anyway?"

"Around," Obie said, wondering what they'd do if they knew how many centuries he had studied music in Nefandus. He remembered the haunting old chants with their complex melodies.

"I'm telling you, it doesn't matter where you got your lessons," Dacey said. "You're awesome."

Suddenly, Nolo jumped from behind his drum set and joined them. "Look who's coming."

The club owner, Guy Keyes, a short man with a large diamond earring, walked over to them, carrying a stack of white papers. He had put on too much bronze tanning cream, and his skin had taken on an orange tint. He was followed by a steroid-pumped guy in a black turtleneck who was trying too hard to look hip.

Nolo hungrily took the papers and started reading. "We have got to get an agent," he said, almost moaning.

"It's just a boilerplate contract, boys," Mr. Keyes said and held out a thick, green pen. "It's the one I offer all the performers here."

"No way," Dacey yanked the contract from Nolo's hands. "We're not signing anything. They'll make a fortune off us while we're stuck playing here for eternity."

"So what?" Obie said. He was anxious for something steady so he could help pay the bills.

"Let's just sign it," Les said and pointed to the figures inked into the blanks. "Read the bottom line."

Dacey whistled, then grabbed the pen and scrawled his name across the back page with a dramatic flourish. Les, Nolo, and Obie signed on the remaining lines.

"Thanks, boys," Mr. Keyes said and folded

the pages. "I'll call you on Monday." He raised his chubby hand, and, as if a technician had been waiting for the sign, the houselights went out. The laser lights began to fill the room with colored patterns, flashing in time with the pounding beat.

"Tonight, you've got to celebrate with us," Dacey said, and put his arm around Obie.

"Sure." Obie agreed reluctantly. Between sets, he'd heard enough about their party the night before. If he wanted to get zombied out on drugs, all he had to do was go back to Nefandus and become Master Hawkwick's *servus* again. "Where are we going?"

"Private party down in Malibu," Les put in. "Everyone's going to be there."

Obie nodded, but then he glimpsed Allison, dancing by herself, her hips moving slow and inviting, her bare back smooth and tanned.

"I'll catch you guys later," Obie said and handed his guitar to Skyler.

Les laughed. "I told you a girl was messing up your mind."

Obie ignored him and jumped off the stage. He landed with a heavy thump, then wiped the bottom edge of his shirt over his face. He felt guilty for the way he had treated Allison. He wasn't even sure why he had been so rude.

Girls grabbed at him. Their hands brushed over his arms, soft and caressing, their eyes flirtatious, trying to make him stay.

"I loved your music," one said and boldly danced against him. She had golden flecks on her cheeks and a glossy smile.

Obie realized then that he should have asked Berto or Kyle to show him how to dance. He felt stiff. He tried to imitate the girl, but that only made the others laugh. He glided away, searching for Allison. At last he found her.

"I think it's my turn to apologize," he said against her ear.

She flinched and turned, surprised to see him. Was it only the flashing light that made her look so angry?

Allison turned her back on him and started dancing again, her hips moving sensually. He wasn't sure if her movement were an invitation, or a brush-off. After all, she had turned her back to Sledge when she had danced with him.

"I mean, I wish I had accepted your apology. It was rude of me not to." He tentatively touched her waist the way he had seen Sledge do.

She recoiled, her eyes darting around the club. Was she hoping Sledge would rescue her, or was she afraid Sledge had seen them together?

But before Obie could think it through, huge hands grabbed his shoulders, spun him around and pushed him hard.

"What are you doing?" Sledge yelled above the music.

Obie stumbled back and fell against the dancers. A girl cried out and hopped on one foot. Obie started to lunge at Sledge, but Kyle suddenly appeared as if he had been watching and stepped between them.

"Just walk away," Kyle said to Obie. "You don't want to fight here and get the band fired."

Obie nodded, then turned and pushed through the crowd, shoving around bobbing bodies and swinging arms. Kids sang with the song, and some clapped rhythmically to the beat. Kyle shoved through the clubbers.

Near the door, Obie paused and turned back to Kyle. "I'm going to use the restroom," he said. "Unless..."

"No, not cool to drain your lizard outside," Kyle confirmed. "I'll wait with Berto."

Obie pushed into the restroom, the air a bad mix of disinfectant, cigarette smoke, and urine smells. The door closed behind him and the music became barely audible. He walked across the wet floor to the far urinal.

A faint rustle beneath the steady sound of dripping faucets made him glance over his shoulder. He didn't see anything but the scratching sound grew louder. Could a rat be in the room with him? He looked again and this time stealthy scuffing and whispers came from the last stall.

Instinctive fear took hold and in the same moment a dark, narrow line of runic letters scraped across the tile floor, advancing quickly and leaving a trail of black smoke and flame.

The smell of magic spewed into the air, foul and moldering with the scent of evil.

He stared down in disbelief and knew he was in trouble. This time the energy in the inscription had been infused with horrible power. The razor-sharp edges of the ancient writing cut across the ceramic floor with an ear-piercing screech that made chills race up his spine. He started to read the words aloud but stopped. The spoken spell burned his mouth and lips. What would have happened if he had completed the divination?

As before the incantation had been sent to kidnap him. He knew that much, but who would try to pull him back to his own time? He wanted to go home, but definitely not this way. He thought of Inna, but she wouldn't need to cast a spell, and he doubted she would conjure the power of dark forces anyway.

His heart hammered. Even if he ran to the door now, he couldn't get there before the magic lashed around him. Escape was impossible. He tired to remember what his mother had told him. Always in such a spell, part of the sorcerer traveled with it, like a magical remote control, to guide the inscription to the intended victim. The sorcerer could see what the words saw and feel what the letters felt.

Obie smiled, suddenly sure, and as the incantation approached the urinal, he turned and relieved himself over the writing. A hellish scream echoed around him, followed by cursing in his native tongue. The hex evaporated into hissing, foul smoke, and dispersed across the room with terrible omen as the bathroom door opened and Sledge, Forrest and Barry stepped inside. They stood watching Obie, their fists clenched. Then, with a menacing look, Sledge took a slow threatening step forward. He seemed eager to fight.

CHAPTER THIRTEEN

OBIE ZIPPED UP his jeans and spun around. At another time he would have taken on all three, but he couldn't risk losing the band's contract. And that was only part of it now. He didn't want to be distracted in a brawl if the sorcerer sent another spell. He was more afraid of the sorcery than of cracking his skull on the ceramic fixtures.

"I can't fight you," he said, choking out the words. He hated playing the coward, but right now he had no choice.

"You don't have to if you don't want to," Forrest said and started toward him, pushing in the stall doors to make sure they were alone. The soles of his tennis shoes made wet sloshing sounds on the moist tiles.

"But that doesn't mean we're not going to pound you." Sledge stepped forward, flexing his jaw.

Obie froze. His stomach knotted. Kyle had warned him not to use the powers he had been given as a *servus* in Nefandus, but he had never said anything about rune magic. Obie's heartbeat quickened. Did he dare? He wasn't a master like his mother. His craft was barely competent, but he needed only something small to distract Forrest, Sledge, and Barry while he got away. He took a deep breath and marked the air, trying to remember the spell for peace. His hand slashed down, then with a flourish came up, scratching out the letters. But even though he had written the incantation, nothing happened.

"What are you doing?" Sledge demanded angrily, but Barry looked fascinated.

"It must be some martial-arts move," Forrest added and assumed an odd pose; he held his hands up like two striking cobras, then his leg flung out and he kicked high.

Obie stepped back, dodging the heel of Forrest's shoe, then he remembered the urinals behind him and jumped forward again. He squinted, trying to recall the right spell.

"He's so freaking weird," Sledge said and slammed his fist into his cupped hand.

"Maybe," Barry muttered. "He could be trying to disappear again."

"Would you get off it?" Sledge said angrily. "He can't go invisible."

"I know what I saw," Barry argued. "We should be trying to make friends with him and find out where he's from."

"You had too much beer to drink and the glare screwed with your vision," Forrest said, siding with Sledge, as always.

While they were arguing, Obie edged sideways.

"Grab him," Sledge ordered, and Forrest closed in.

But before either could throw a punch, Obie wagged his finger and wrote a different inscription for peace. This time the letters glowed and hung in the air before diffusing and misting over Sledge, Forrest and Barry.

"Did he spray something on us?" Sledge asked, and spit as if he had a foul taste in his mouth.

"What the—?" Forrest wiped his face and sneezed.

Then Barry waved his fingers through the floating gold flecks and froze, his hand still reaching up. Sledge and Forest paused, befuddled, and immediately their eyes glazed over as if in a trance. All three stood rigid like department-store mannequins.

The spell must have been one that tranquilized, rather than an incantation to make peace. He had to get away before the magic evaporated, but he couldn't just leave them, transfixed and staring at the blocks of disinfectant in the bottom of the urinals.

At last he took a deep breath and sliced the air, marking *wunjo*, for joy, hoping its blessing would release them from his first spell and, at the same time, make them happy enough to forget about beating him up. The letter hovered in front of Obie, then burst into flames as the thick smell of roses permeated the air. Obie knew in an instant he had cast something too powerful. He tried to take it back, but his hand brushed through warm ash. What had he done this time? He waited, terrified, his heart thumping wildly.

At once, Sledge turned with a silly smile on his face. He wiped at the gray soot on his face and started undulating as if he were boneless.

The door opened and Kyle peeked in. "What's taking you so—" His eyes widened and his mouth dropped open in horror.

Sledge, Barry, and Forrest were dancing and singing raucous verses of some locker-room song, moving their heads exaggeratedly, then swirling and swooping dangerously close to the urinals.

"What the heck did you do to them?" Kyle asked and his lips closed in a strange grimace, as if he were trying to suppress a smile.

"I didn't want to fight them," Obie explained. "But they were determined."

"Let's take the stage!" Sledge yelled, and pushed between Obie and Kyle.

"Obie's not the only one with talent," Forrest said and ran after Sledge.

Barry whooped and joined them.

Kyle stood in front of Obie, barring his exit. "So, what exactly did you do to them? I sure hope you're not going to tell me you gave them something illegal."

"I thought I was casting a spell for joy," Obie explained.

"A spell?" Kyle stared at him with the same uneasy look he got when he watched Obie eat raw meat.

"I used magic," Obie confessed.

Kyle leaned against the door and let his head fall back. "Magic? I thought you said there was nothing special about you."

"My mother was a rune master," Obie explained. "I was never really good with runic inscriptions. I think I cast something to make their inhibitions break down."

Laughter boomed from the other room and the music stopped.

"Man, we'd better go see what they're doing." Kyle turned and pushed through the door.

By the time Kyle and Obie reached the dance floor, the houselights were up and the DJ had put on a disco song. Sledge, Forrest, and Barry stood together on stage in a line, snapping their fingers and nodding their heads with the beat; then, without warning they slid their feet apart, bending their knees, and in unison they tucked their hands into their armpits as if they were making wings. They flapped their elbows and kicked back, first with one leg and then with the other.

The music blared louder. Kids burst out laughing, then started chanting, "Go, Sledge! Go, Forrest! Go, Barry!"

"I haven't seen anyone do the Funky Chicken since my grandpa got drunk at my aunt's wedding," the DJ said into his microphone.

"I hope you can remember a spell for forgetfulness," Kyle said and shook his head.

"Because if they remember this, they are going to be gunning for you. Let's go."

Obie turned to follow Kyle but then he saw Allison. She held up her camera and took one last picture of him.

He walked over to her. "For someone who hates wannabe rock stars, you focused on me tonight."

"If you think I'm interested in you, forget it," she said in a haughty tone. "That's not what it means."

"Then why were you taking so many photographs of me?" Obie asked, hating her insolent tone.

"Barry asked me to. He wanted candid shots of you, from every angle." She turned with a derisive scowl and walked away.

Obie's heart lurched. He hurried to the door and pushed his way outside.

"I think I've got a big problem," Obie said when he joined Berto and Kyle.

"What is it now?" Kyle asked, his eyes rolling in utter disbelief. "Please don't tell me there's more."

"I think Barry saw me disappear," Obie admitted, and quickly told Kyle and Berto what had happened at the poultry shop.

"So what?" Kyle said when he had finished. "They've got no proof. Who cares if Allison has a few dozen pictures of you? It's just a big waste of film." He smiled. "I'm going home and picking up the shoes I promised to deliver for the early-morning call. I'll catch up with you at Pink's." He started away.

As soon as Kyle had gone down the street, Berto nudged Obie. "What weren't you telling Kyle?" he asked. "What's going to show up in those pictures?"

"My new shoes hurt," Obie began slowly. "And it was dark onstage, so I let my feet turn to shadow to since I couldn't take the pain. I guess I was too into playing music to notice Allison taking all those pictures. And now she'll see . . ."

Berto gave Obie a devious look. "It's a simple fix. We'll break into Allison's house and steal her film, but we have to do something big as a cover so she won't notice it's missing."

Obie listened to Berto's plan, somehow knowing that the evening was going to become even stranger.

CHAPTER FOURTEEN

BERTO WAITED FOR OBIE at the corner of Hollywood and Vine. Red roses were bundled in burlap on the sidewalk beside him and packages of chocolate kisses bulged from a brown shopping bag.

"Allison is home now," Obie said, feeling nervous about their plan. "But I don't know which room is hers."

"It doesn't matter," Berto said with assurance. He scooped up the roses and handed them to Obie.

"But what if she's in bed?" Obie asked, his arms so jittery the rose petals trembled.

"Then we'll be quiet so we don't wake her up," Berto answered.

"I don't like this," Obie said. "It feels wrong."

"All you have to do is lay out flowers and candy while I steal the film," Berto explained for the fourth time.

"Won't she wonder how we got inside?" Obie asked.

"She won't know we did it," Berto said confidently. "She'll think it was Sledge, and when he says he didn't, her mind will be so preoccupied trying to figure out who it was that she won't even notice her film is missing."

"All right, then," Obie agreed at last.

Berto started to fade; his arms became ill defined and his face blurred. When Obie didn't follow him, he became solid again. "What's wrong?"

"I can't turn to shadow when I'm nervous," Obie explained. "The adrenaline or something makes my muscles too tense. I have to feel relaxed."

Berto shook his head as if he thought Obie

were pathetic. "I don't care what Kyle's been telling you," Berto said candidly. "You need to practice. What are you going to do if some bounty hunter comes after you?"

"I don't know," Obie said and drew long breaths, expanding his lungs and hoping to calm his nerves. At last his skin bristled and became foggy. Then his body drifted out, forming a long, smoky puff. The breeze murmured through him, and he fluttered upward. Berto waited for him, a jet-black cloud beneath an awning.

Together they skimmed over the silvery tops of palm trees and continued, two dark streaks, to the back of the guitar shop. They found an open window, then spread themselves thin and squeezed through the tarnished screen. Their shadows vibrated against the metal mesh, making a peculiar, buzzing sound.

The taste of rust and dirt filled Obie's mouth as he materialized in the dark on the second floor near the stairs. His stomach burned with nerves, and a new worry seized him. How was he going to explain his prowling to Allison, or her mother, if one of them caught him standing in their home like a half-witted burglar holding a bouquet of roses?

"Go," Berto whispered harshly, nudging him forward.

The living room opened into the dinning room; a long counter divided both rooms from the kitchen. Obie crossed to a hallway. The sound of running water came from behind the first door. He imagined Allison in the shower, her hands catching the spray, rubbing her body—he shook his head, trying to rid himself of the image, and hurried forward, the velvety petals brushing softly against his nose and chin.

He glanced into the first room and barely made out a bed and a computer. He was sure the bedroom didn't belong to Allison, because even over the fragrance of the roses in his arms he smelled something sour, a curious mix of licorice and tobacco.

"That's got to be her brother's room," Obie said. He hadn't thought Allison had a brother.

Obie peered through the next doorway and

immediately recognized Allison's clothes on the floor. When he was confident the room was empty, he went inside and waited, then closed the door behind Berto before he flicked on the light. Black-and-white photos of Allison and her father covered one wall. Scarves, purses, caps, and jewelry hung from hooks on the other.

Berto grabbed Allison's camera off her dresser, opened it, and tore out the film. "How many pictures did she take?"

"Thirty, or forty, maybe. I don't know," Obie said, trying to remember. He took the burlap off the roses and started placing them around the room.

"There's got to be more rolls someplace," Berto whispered, opening a drawer. His hands rifled through Allison's bras and panties, searching.

Obie stared stupidly.

Berto turned and caught him. "What?"

"How are we going to explain this if we get caught?" Obie asked.

"We won't get caught," Berto muttered and closed the drawer.

Obie nodded. He felt oddly dizzy, as if all his blood had drained to his feet, and he couldn't breathe.

"Set some flowers on her bed," Berto ordered in a hushed tone.

A tangle of zebra-print sheets and blankets curled over Allison's mattress. Obie placed the roses across her pillow. His hand tentatively caressed the fabric where he thought her head must have lain. Then he drew his hand back in anger. What made him so infatuated with her? She was rude and arrogant—

"Hurry," Berto interrupted his thoughts.

Obie dropped the flowers in a big lump, then grabbed a bag of candy, tore it open and, shaking out the pieces, formed a trail of chocolate kisses from the bed to the door. When he reached the entrance to her room, he poured out the contents of three more bags; then he tenderly shaped the silver-wrapped candies into a large heart.

Berto opened the last drawer and pulled out two rolls of film. He showed them to Obie, then stuffed them in his pocket.

The water stopped. Silence followed. Obie glanced up.

"It's okay," Berto whispered and stepped around Obie. "I'll stand lookout in the hallway."

Obie emptied the last bag of chocolate kisses on the floor, but he couldn't concentrate. His mind filled with images of Allison stepping onto the rug in front of the shower, grabbing a towel and drying off, her long hair wet and falling over her shoulders. He didn't notice the soft swish of footsteps on the rug until a drop of water fell on his head, followed quickly by another.

"Allison?" He glanced back at the wide, bare foot behind him. Coarse black hair jutted from the fat toes. The nails were split and yellowed. Obie jumped up, turned, and stood face to face with a huge, naked man.

CHAPTER FIFTEEN

OBIE PUSHED AROUND the man, his fingers accidentally brushing over thick rolls of wet, warm flesh. Berto waited in the dark for him, holding his sides, and trying hard not to laugh.

"Some lookout you turned out to be!" Obie hissed angrily, and he sprinted toward the stairs.

Berto grabbed his shoulders and pulled him back. "What are you doing?" Berto asked. "Just fade."

"I can't," Obie said, and dropped the bag of candy still clenched in his hand. Chocolate kisses scattered across the rug. He sucked in deep breaths, trying to push back the panic. "I'm too nervous."

"What are you two doing in my house?!" the man yelled as he wrapped a terry-cloth robe around his mammoth body and pounded after them.

"Are you sure we got the right place?" Berto asked, barely able to speak through his chuckling.

As if in answer, Allison's voice came from downstairs. "Grandpa, are you all right?"

"That's Allison," Obie said, alarmed. His heart sank. "We're trapped."

"She hasn't seen you yet." Berto grasped Obie's arm. "Just relax, and I'll make you disappear with me."

"Call the cops!" Allison's grandfather yelled.

Berto concentrated, but nothing happened. "I can't make you turn to shadow, either." He released Obie and looked surprised. "That's never happened to me before. We'll have to run for it."

Footsteps sounded on the stairs. "Grandpa!"

Allison called, her voice closer, and this time her mother joined in. "Dad, what's going on up there?"

In the same moment, Allison's grandfather opened a closet, picked up a golf club and came toward Berto and Obie, swinging wildly. The iron head hit the wall with a loud clatter, and plaster scattered around the old man.

"Your choice," Berto said. "We can either fight Grandpa, or dodge past Allison."

Obie let out a muffled cry, yanked his T-shirt over his face, and ran down the stairs, the thundering racket of Berto's footsteps behind him. He bumped into Allison and her mother, then squeezed between them.

Allison stopped. "Obie?" she cried out.

Her mother gasped. "What are you doing here, Obie?"

"Sorry!" he shouted back, and dropped his shirt. He leaped over the last four steps. "It's not what you think."

"Stop them!" Allison's grandfather shouted.

"Obie, what were you doing to my grandfather?" Allison screamed.

Berto pushed between Allison and her mother, taking the stairs two at a time. "Everything's fine, ladies," Berto said, and laughed before continuing, "The guy's just expressing what's in his heart."

Obie stopped, and Berto rammed into him. "Why did you say that?"

"We'll discuss it later, all right?" Berto said. "I think Grandpa's calling the cops."

Obie dashed down the back hallway. At the door leading to the parking lot, he tried to push back the bolt, but his fingers were shaking so badly he couldn't grasp the knob. At last he slid it aside and opened the door, banging it against the wall, and he raced across the asphalt, his footsteps echoing into the night.

A few blocks later, he slowed down. Berto caught up to him and burst out laughing.

"Why did you tell them that?" Obie lunged, but Berto dodged.

"Weren't you expressing your heart?" Berto teased. "I think you like Allison. You talk about her all the time."

Obie kicked at the sidewalk, scuffing his

toe. "How am I ever going to explain this?" he said, fuming.

Berto snorted, and wiped at the tears streaming down his face. "Don't bother," he said and climbed on his motorcycle. "You're so busted, they're never going to believe anything you tell them, anyway."

Obie groaned in embarrassment. He swung his leg over the bike and settled in behind Berto, his feet on the pegs. The bike blasted away, and the cold air slapped his face. Suddenly Berto gave the bike extra throttle and pulled back on the handlebars, popping a wheelie. He hollered with joy, exhilarated.

The front wheel bounced down and Obie bit the side of his mouth. He sat motionless and glum, the engine vibrating through him, and wished he were alone back at the loft so he could pull apart all his misery and study it piece by piece. Maybe it had been a mistake for him to leave Nefandus after all. He was never going to fit into this world.

A few minutes later, Berto pulled up in front of Pink's hot dog stand and got off the bike. He waited on the curb for Obie, his eyes bright and energetic. "Everyone who's into the L.A. nightlife comes here for a dog," he said. "The place is always jammed."

Obie reluctantly followed him and joined the crowd waiting in line, but he couldn't get his mind on the menu. Even the aroma of spicy chili and fresh, steaming hot dog buns didn't pull him out of his mood.

Berto paid, picked up their food and carried it to a table.

Obie slid into a chair beside him. The autographed, glossy photos of celebrities covered the wall above them, seeming to stare down at Obie, mocking him.

"Eat," Berto said, chewing. "You won't feel like such a complete loser then." He snickered and wiped mustard from his lips.

Obie glowered and took a bite. The hot dog popped, filling his mouth with garlicky flavor.

"There's Kyle." Berto waved.

Kyle stood at the entrance, looking worried. He saw them, hurried over to their table and sat down. "Sledge is out driving around, looking for you. He said you broke into Allison's house. I didn't believe him—"

Berto laughed uncontrollably and sprayed food over the table.

Obie quickly explained everything that had happened. When he finished, he added, "At least we got the film."

Kyle leaned back in his chair and brushed his hand over the top of his head. "The way you're both acting, you're going to get caught, and if not by a bounty hunter, then by someone from the *National Enquirer*. And that's worse. Do you want a reporter to find out about Nefandus and go in there on an expedition? All hell, literally, will break loose."

"No one saw us turn into shadow," Berto said tensely, pushing his hot dog away. "And it's not like anyone is going to figure out how to get into Nefandus, anyway."

"You guys don't get it," Kyle said. "There are ancient references to Nefandus, but right now scholars don't believe them, the same way they once didn't think the stories about Troy were true. But if they have any proof at all, people will try to go there."

Kyle paused, then added, "I think we should lay down some new rules."

Berto stood abruptly. "You're making life impossible. We did the right thing tonight." He glared at Kyle, his face flushed in anger, daring him to argue. "Maybe I should go back to Nefandus. It was easier than living here with you and all your rules." He tromped out.

A few minutes, later the heavy growl of his motorcycle shuddered through the night.

Anger simmered inside Obie. "You're too hard on Berto," Obie ventured. "And on me. If something happens to Berto, it'll be your fault."

"His outbursts are just for show," Kyle said. "He won't go back. He's threatened that before, and even if he did, we both know it was only a matter of time. His dark side is too strong."

"He's trying to control it," Obie defended Berto. "You're not being fair."

"Fair?" Kyle said, tensely. "Both of you expect me to shoulder all the responsibility, and

I'm sick of it. I fit in here, and I'm tired of babysitting two Renegades." He stood. "Get caught. I could care less."

Kyle walked out.

Another time, Obie might have gone after Kyle and tried to smooth things out, but he was tired now. He considered his options. Dacey had offered to let him move in with him. Maybe it was time to leave. He only had a few things he needed to pick up at the loft.

He left his food and walked down Melrose Avenue, then took a sidestreet and started running. When he was up to speed, he dived, dissolving as he did, and expecting to soar on the wind, but something hard slammed against him. He fell to the concrete and his body snapped tightly back together.

CHAPTER SIXTEEN

OBIE HIT THE SIDEWALK and skidded, scraping his palms on the concrete. His chin struck a sprinkler head, and pain shot through his neck, skating down his spine. He rolled over and looked up, disoriented.

Barry and Forrest towered over him. Sledge paced on the lawn, his feet crackling over dead leaves, the toe of his shoe perilously close to Obie's head.

"What were you thinking, going over to Allison's house tonight?" Sledge asked gruffly.

Forrest and Barry grabbed Obie's arms and yanked him to his feet. Obie staggered, but they held him tightly between them. He didn't struggle. He calmed his mind and steadied his nerves.

"What kind of drug did you spray on us back at the club?" Sledge yelled.

"Magic," Obie whispered insolently.

"Hold him." Sledge lumbered forward and swung.

Obie didn't flinch. When the punch grazed his chin, he disappeared in a *poof.*

Sledge's fist smashed through the air, and inertia propelled him forward. He lost his balance and stumbled, caught himself, and whipped around. "I told you two to hold onto him."

Forrest didn't answer. He stood slack-faced, then grabbed at his throat, hyperventilating.

"Where did he go?" Sledge spun around again as though his mind couldn't accept what his eyes had witnessed. Perspiration broke out across his forehead, and then he plopped onto the lawn, his legs seemingly too weak to hold himself upright.

Barry stared up at the sky, awestruck. "He disappeared," he said, a fine quiver in his voice. "I told you what I saw before." He waved his trembling fingers through the air where Obie had stood moments before.

Obie circled back, a blur of fog. The metallic taste of their fear permeated him. He didn't want them to know about his strange abilities yet. He had other plans for them now. He lingered, a phantom, and tried to remember the incantation for forgetfulness. The word puffed from his spectral shape and spilled into the night like fairy dust.

Barry blinked and wiped his face.

"What was that?" Sledge shuddered and spit.

"Maybe a floating spiderweb," Forest said and sneezed.

"Come on." Sledge stood and started walking back to Barry's car, as if nothing out of the ordinary had happened. "We're never going to find Obie here. Let's head to Chinatown."

"I'm craving some dim sum anyway," Barry agreed, pulling the keys from his pocket.

Obie sighed. He wasn't going to live with Kyle; that meant he no longer had to go to school. Those three wouldn't be bothering him anymore.

He soared, a black spiral, toward the L.A. skyline. His senses were awakened, and the darkness inside him became stronger. The evil he had suppressed for so long pulsed freely through him. He'd been naive and stupid. He could control his fate, and not be its victim. Why had he wasted precious time trying to fit in with those foolish mortals, when he could have used his magic and ruled them?

Maybe there had been a time when he had been one of them, but that was long ago. Too much of his humanity had been lost living in Nefandus. He had centuries of evil memories to rely on, so why should he even try to be good now?

Over Chinatown, he condensed himself into near-human form and dove toward the loft apartment. He was anxious to shrug off Kyle and his rules. He fumed out again and drifted to the ground, then re-formed in full light, no longer caring who might see. Let them witness his power and fear him.

He wanted only a few things; the helle rune and the music he had been writing. He ignored the low rustle in the bougainvillea behind him. Maybe it was only a breeze, but if it were a predator stirring through the twiggy branches, Obie was ready; he felt ruthless and cat-quick. He turned the doorknob.

A soft hand curled over his. "You're acting foolish, Omer."

"Inna?" He whipped around, startled, and his excruciating loneliness came back, harsher and more intense than his evil.

She appeared beside him, her body still transparent and forming, her cloak wavering, a golden mist behind her. The runic inscription on her bracelet blazed. She smiled softly as if she understood what he had been through, and loved him anyway.

"Time is running out," she whispered.

Suddenly the goodness inside him burst forth. "I was good once, Inna," he whispered with intense regret. "Take me back," he pleaded. "I don't fit into this world. If I stay here, I'm afraid of what I'll do. Just now the darkness in me became too strong.

The things I wanted to do..." He let the words fall away, ashamed. "I need to leave. Give me the right incantation so I can return with you."

"You belong here, Omer," Inna said gently. A dagger now hung next to her leather pouch, from a thick rope that encircled her waist. He wondered what danger she had left behind in her own time.

"I don't belong here," he argued, his chest tightening with piercing pain. "I don't fit in. I've tried."

"I've always known your destiny wasn't with me, but here, with another," she whispered, her eyes fervent. "The day I agreed to marry you, your mother came to me and confessed what she had done to save your life."

"She never told me," Obie said, baffled.

"You're one of the Four of Legend, and you can't waste time fighting with those who share your future."

"Kyle?" he said. He tried to remember the legend, but if he had ever known the story, it was lost to him now.

Inna held up her hand, signaling him to be silent. She looked nervously around, as if something had frightened her, and suddenly Obie felt his own heart stop. Inna was afraid. He could see fear in her eyes, but it was not for herself—it was for him.

"You have to go back to Nefandus and steal back your mother's runes," she spoke quickly.

"My mother's runes lost their power the day she died," Obie countered. "And my father hid them with her, in a secret burial mound."

"Stop thinking, and use your senses," Inna ordered, "to know what I say is true."

Obie paused. His father had told him to trust his intuition. In battle, his senses were keener than his thoughts. If he tried to outthink his opponent, he always lost. He had to rely on a deeper intelligence. Obie let his mind go still, and the chattering doubts stopped. In that second, he experienced pure trust in Inna. A quiet peace settled over him.

But then, without warning, he also felt something dreadful. An overwhelming and instinctive fear rushed through him. The atmosphere seemed filled with conflicting incantations, as if two sources of magic were fighting, one coming toward him, and the other trying to bar its approach. Had that discord always been around him?

"You must have your mother's runes to fulfill your destiny," Inna explained. Her brow grew furrowed, and she held her fingers to the breeze as if sensing something.

"What is it?" Obie asked, and as he spoke the air shifted.

The night became quiet, and time seemed to decelerate. The streetlights dimmed, and even the fuchsia-colored blossoms, falling from the bougainvillea, appeared to defy gravity and flutter too slowly to the ground.

Obie touched Inna, fearful that he would never see her again. His hands held a memory of their own and his fingers slid down her slender back and drew her close to him.

Her body felt real to his touch, and radiated

warmth, but he knew she was only an illusion. He pulled her back beneath the vine, until they were hidden in a deeper shadow under the trellis. He kissed her, freely, knowing he could not harm her with the darkness that lingered inside him, because she was no more than a beguiling specter, formed by magic. He breathed in the familiar scent of her hair, the freshness of pine needles, and the smoke from campfires.

"Take me with you," he whispered again. "Even if I did find my mother's runes, I wouldn't know how to work them. My powers are weak. I'm a warrior, not a sorcerer."

"You're not aware yet. Others want your power and will do anything to gain it," Inna said softly, her lips moving across his neck. Suddenly, she pulled away from him, and her eyes widened, searching.

The air rippled around her with a golden cast, and the runic letters on her bracelet dissolved and, like fine sand, spilled to the ground.

"Something has followed me," she said, frantic. "It's broken my spell. Go quickly! Leave!"

Inna's mouth opened as if to say something more, but she shattered, breaking into pieces of blinding white light.

"Inna!" Obie screamed, trying to catch her.

The fierce brightness faded, replaced by a peculiar and suffocating heaviness. The air became filled with the carrion stench that lingered over a battlefield, but this smell came from something corrupt and evil that was trying to envelop him. He thought he caught movement out of the corner of his eye, but when he looked again it was gone. Only gnarled vines and the rungs of a trellis filled the deepening shadows.

Wary, he stepped back, flat against the thorny limbs, his heart pounding. He suppressed an urge to run and waited, hoping this time to identify his enemy. A weird certainty came over him. Something evil was stalking him and trying to abduct him. He could feel its presence, but another force, benign and equally strong, was barring it from touching him.

The night remained oddly silent, as the two

powers dueled. Then, suddenly, the fragrance of burning roses overwhelmed the scent of decay and corpses, and whatever danger had been there vanished, as if some fragile deadlock had been reached. He stepped from his hiding place, his heartbeat slowing, and gazed at the starry sky. The strange, overpowering feeling of menace was gone now, and the wind resumed, rustling through his hair.

CHAPTER SEVENTEEN

ALONE IN HIS ROOM, Obie stretched across the bed and stared at the ceiling, waiting for dawn, undecided and queasy. The iguana scuttled back and forth across his chest in sudden quick stops and starts, seeking warmth, but when he petted its leathery body, it twisted its head, then scurried away, leaving him to his thoughts.

He tried to recall the Legend of the Four, but he couldn't concentrate; his mind kept returning to what Inna had said about retrieving his mother's rune stones. He realized now that all his threats of returning to Nefandus had been foolish bravado. He didn't want to go back.

Hazy memories of his aunt Shatri came to him. She had taken him into Nefandus after his father's murder, to protect him from the Haliurunnae. But the evil environment there had leached all kindness from her, and when he had refused to show her his mother's grave, she had given him to Hawkwick as a *servus*. He felt certain his aunt had the runes now, but why would she want them? Their magic had died with his mother.

At last Obie fell into a fitful sleep. He dreamed again of his father and the sword thrust through his heart. In the nightmare he grasped the hilt and tried to pull the blade from his chest. The runic inscriptions ran swiftly back and forth over the metal, and even though Obie held on tight, he wasn't stronger than the magic.

The inscription was divided by arcane symbols he didn't understand, but the rhyming pattern of the incantation he knew well. The language was never meant to be spoken, but in his dream he muttered the words. The first two syllables rhymed, followed by a third that rhymed with the next word.

The harsh smell of smoke awakened Obie, and he turned, thinking he had slept in the forest near a campfire, but the mattress smelled of soap and bleach, not earth and pine needles. He opened his eyes and stared at the flat, white walls. The smoke alarm went off, and the shrill, ear-piercing sound snapped him out of his dream state. He kicked off his blankets, jumped up, and ran to the kitchen, the concrete floor cold against his bare feet, and then he stopped, stunned by what he saw.

Smoke plumed from the cast-iron pan, the blue flame still blazing underneath. The food had turned to charcoal, and the fire had left a ring of soot on the stove.

Obie started to move around the counter, but an unsettling feeling made him pause. His senses bristled, warning him of danger. The room felt odd, the atmosphere inharmoniously heavy, and underneath the thick smoke he caught a whiff of something putrid and foul.

His heart began to pound. He stared anxiously at the black skillet, wondering if Berto had concocted a sacrifice for his god, Tezcatlipoca, lord of the smoking mirror, and something had gone terribly wrong.

He glanced about him. The iguana sat lazily at the window, basking in the morning sunshine. Dirty dishes were piled in the sink. A carton of milk sat on the counter along with a five-pound sack of masa harina and a carton of eggs. Maybe Berto had gone off and forgotten to turn off the burner, but Obie sensed that something much worse had happened.

"What are you doing?" Kyle ran into the kitchen, hopping into his jeans. He looked shaken, his eyes still blinking away sleep. He grabbed a chair, stood on it, and turned off the smoke alarm.

The silence that followed was tense. Obie tried hard not to recall his anger from the night before. He remembered Inna's words and stared at Kyle, wondering what bound their destinies.

Kyle, marched over to the stove and turned

the knob beneath the burner. The flame went out. "When the food burns," he said condescendingly, "you turn off the fire."

"Something happened to Berto," Obie said, no longer willing to carry on their fighting.

"Nothing happened to him. He does stuff like this all the time." Kyle looked around the kitchen assessing the amount of work it would take to clean up. "He astral-projects or dreamwalks, whatever you want to call that creepy thing he does, and just leaves."

Obie turned, not wanting to listen to Kyle, and as he did, he caught furtive movement on the floor near the refrigerator. He stepped closer, and fear seized him. A chain of interlocking runic letters slipped stealthily toward him, forming a ring large enough to ensnare him.

"Someone sent an incantation and abducted Berto," Obie said and cautiously knelt. The stench of evil was much stronger now. He quickly scanned the writing and recognized the peculiar flourish of the letters *raido* and *thurisaz*. He knew that his aunt Shatri had sent the spell.

But then he noticed more; the familiar pattern he had seen on the sword in his nightmare of his father's murder. He froze. His lungs forgot to breathe, and blood surged through his ears. He struggled against the knowledge; he didn't want to believe. But within the coiling inscription, two syllables rhymed, followed by a third that rhymed with a syllable in the next word. Decorative symbols were drawn in between, to hide the true incantation. This was the same style of the spell that had been cast to kill his father.

Hot, stinging tears welled up, and Obie blinked them away. His aunt Shatri had murdered his father. He never would have suspected her, because she hadn't had the physical strength to fight King Filimer. No one had. But magic had empowered her and given her the victory.

Everything that had happened following his father's death suddenly made sense. Aunt Shatri had not wanted to protect Obie from the Haliurunnae; she had wanted to get him away from his tribe of Visigoths before he uncovered the truth. But what had she wanted from him? She could have killed him easily, too, so there must have been some reason to keep him alive—but what?

"It's nothing," Kyle interrupted his thoughts. He stood over Obie and looked down at the rotating words. "You and Berto need to dump all your superstitious nonsense." He started to slip his bare toe into the circle to prove Obie wrong.

Obie grabbed Kyle's ankle, stopping him.

"If you won't believe me," Obie said. "I'll show you." He stood, walked to the window, picked up the iguana, and then carefully shoved the squirming lizard into the middle of the circling words.

The iguana vanished.

Kyle stared, stunned, then looked at Obie. "Where did it go?"

"Back to Nefandus," Obie said, his stomach churning. "My aunt Shatri has used this to capture Berto. He's her prisoner now. We have to go find him."

"How?" Kyle said, his voice strained.

"That's like saying you're going to find a friend who's lost someplace in L.A. We wouldn't even know where to start, and you still don't even know that that's where he is. Maybe the circle just makes him disappear."

"Can't you trust anything I say?" Obie clenched his hand, infuriated. He didn't want to argue anymore; he wanted to slam his fist into Kyle's face. "If my aunt has kidnapped him, then she has done it to make me come to her. Berto will be at her house, and,if you're too afraid to save a friend, I'll go alone. I'm not a coward."

The incantation smoldered and disappeared.

Obie turned and left the kitchen before Kyle could respond.

Kyle's bare feet slapped the concrete floor, following after him. "You can't go like this. You need to think first and make a plan."

Obie's his anger burst forth. "Don't say another word to me," he said, threateningly. His hand rose and then fell to his side with a loud *thwack*. "I'm through talking to you."

An odd pallor covered Kyle's face. He had seen a danger in Obie's eyes that hadn't been there before.

Obie went to his room, yanked his clothes up from the floor and hurriedly put them on. He picked up the hellerune and slipped it into his jeans pocket. He had thought Kyle would change his mind, and it bothered him that he hadn't. He didn't want his destiny entwined with a weakling who wouldn't risk his life to save that of another.

He tied back his hair, determined, and then placed his hands flat against the wall and focused his energy. He had the power to go back to Nefandus without using one of the portals. Other Renegades, if they wanted to slip back inside, had to use certain gateways between the two worlds that opened only at specific times, but Obie didn't have to wait. Hawkwick had taught him how to shift between dimensions from any location.

Slowly, the paint began to foam over his fingers, as if he were melding with the building, but the spume was only agitated atoms. Muffled knocking came from far away, and he ignored it. Subdued voices followed.

Obie was already sinking into the boundary between the two dimensions, his body starting to make the transition, when footsteps sounded from down the hall, barely audible, and stopped at his bedroom door.

"Obie," A voice called, breaking his concentration. "What are you doing?" It was Allison.

CHAPTER EIGHTEEN

"ALLISON," OBIE GASPED. Sharp pain exploded through him and he fumbled to make sense of what was happening. He wrenched himself back, and dizziness swept over him as he reconnected to the present world. The wall still rippled, but his room was dark, and he didn't think Allison had noticed.

"Were you meditating?" Allison stood near his bed, staring at him oddly, unable to hide the skittish fear in her eyes. What had she seen?

Obie grinned foolishly; even if Allison hadn't seen him stepping *through* the wall, she had found him pressed tight against it in a peculiar and unbecoming way.

"I was exercising," Obie lied. "Calisthenics. It looks weird, huh?"

She smiled, eager to accept his lie, and relaxed into a more natural stance, raking her hands through her shiny hair.

"I can't really talk right now," Obie said curtly, feeling time rushing away from him. He dashed over to her. "I'm sorry about last night. If you came over to collect your apology, you have it."

She looked up at him, surprised. "That's not exactly the greeting I had expected," she answered flirtatiously. She had clearly spent a long time on her makeup and he wondered if it had been for him; then he remembered Sledge. He was probably waiting for her outside.

He took her elbow and started down the hallway, with long strides.

"I wanted to thank you for the flowers and the chocolate kisses," she said, taking two steps for each one of his. "I thought that was so sweet."

"You're welcome." He quickened his pace. At least that wasn't going to be a problem, but then, with a sudden jolt, he realized it didn't matter anyway. He wasn't going to have a future here.

"Sledge always spends Sunday mornings with his family," Allison said, pulling him back to their conversation. "I thought we could go out for donuts and coffee."

"I can't," he said brusquely, and he opened the door. He escorted her out to the landing. The air smelled stale and was already warming from the morning sun.

She bit her lower lip, obviously not enjoying his dismissal. "Why not?"

"I have other plans." He had already hesitated too long. He impatiently pushed the call button to summon the elevator. The motor whirred overhead, and, seconds later, the big metal doors rumbled open. The two stepped into the cage.

"Things with Sledge aren't what they seem," Allison said carefully, but then her words fell away, as if she were embarrassed. She closed her eyes and rubbed her forehead. "It's complicated. Can't you just have a cup of coffee with me, so I can explain?"

Obie felt his anxiety building. She was talking about luxuriating in the sun and sipping mocha cappuccinos, and he needed to concentrate and fix his mind on. . . . It suddenly occurred to him that he didn't know what he would be facing. Why was his aunt summoning him now? Couldn't she just have appeared to him, the way Inna had? His stomach fluttered nervously, but he had to stifle his anxiety. What good would it do?

"Obie?" Allison called his name. "Are you all right?"

He looked up. The elevator had opened. She had stepped off and was waiting for him.

"Yeah." He barged off the elevator as the door was closing. He followed Allison outside. The spicy aroma of bacon and sausage reminded him he hadn't eaten.

Allison turned and faced him. "Are you playing some weird kind of game with me? I thought the flowers and candy meant you liked me."

"More than anything I want to spend the day with you," he said and glanced down at her pretty, delicate face. He lifted his hand to stroke her hair, then pulled back. Her Toyota was parked down the street. He started walking that way, pulling her with him, his throat tightening with apprehension.

"Why can't you just go with me, then?" she asked, running to keep up with his pace.

He knew his answer could break their fragile truce, but what could he tell her? His shoulders slumped. It didn't matter what he said, because he would never be able to come back here anyway. He turned and held his face to the sun. Nefandus had an artificial sky and weather, and no moon. He'd miss so much that existed here.

"I have plans," he said simply, and wiped his eyes. "Something I can't get out of."

An odd smile curled across her face. "It's Sledge. You're afraid of him, aren't you?"

"Is that what you think?" he asked.

"You're not the only one," she answered. She climbed into her car.

"What does that mean?" He searched her eyes for the truth.

"If you don't have time to have a cup of coffee with me," she said, with a toss of her head, "then it means, none of your business."

He mentally weighed the needs of two friends. "I'm sorry," he whispered, his decision complete, his chest heavy with foreboding.

Allison sat behind the steering wheel, as she looked up at him through the open car window. "Don't make this visit into something it isn't. I was just being friendly."

She turned the key in the ignition, and the engine roared. She gave him a look and drove off.

When the Toyota had disappeared around the corner, he slipped into a walkway between a restaurant and an acupuncture clinic. He concentrated, vaguely aware of footsteps pounding down the sidewalk, probably a Sunday morning jogger.

He pressed against the building and the

wall swelled as if the brick pattern were on the outside of a balloon. Something tugged at his shoulders, as if trying to pull him back, but he was too far into the passing to return then.

He took a deep breath. He wouldn't be able to breathe again until he was in Nefandus. A thin film covered him and clung to his skin like a moist membrane, and then numbness swept through him. He remained paralyzed, as one by one his atoms reconfigured themselves to fit into the next dimension.

Hawkwick had explained that the universe was composed of atoms, but that between those atoms were spaces in which other atoms spun, creating another universe existing concurrently with the first, the two intricately linked and woven together.

Obie waited impatiently. Seconds ticked away. The passing had never taken this long. Maybe he had lost his ability to come and go between the two realms. His chest began to burn, and his heartbeat slowed. Dark clouds pressed into his vision. His uneasiness escalated to panic; he suddenly felt certain he was going to remain imprisoned for eternity in this gluey nowhere world between the two dimensions. Could Shatri have set a trap using Berto, knowing Obie would recklessly charge into Nefandus to rescue his friend?

CHAPTER NINETEEN

AT LAST A DULL throb swept through Obie, and the numbness left him. His shoulders strained as if he had been dragging a heavy weight, and then, without warning, he plunged into Nefandus, and water slapped his face. He gasped, stunned, and for one panicked moment thought he had fallen into a river. He sputtered and blinked, disoriented, then realized he had arrived in the middle of a storm. Cold rain pelted him, stinging like tiny stones. He splashed into deep puddles and ran for shelter, sensing something behind him, but too afraid to turn and look.

Tall, narrow houses lined the streets and, high above him, water gurgled from the mouths of gargoyles projecting from the eaves. He found refuge on a rickety porch and hid in darkness. Runoff spilled around him in an unrelenting thrum, and a familiar fear gathered in his stomach. He wondered what was lurking in the somber, misty shadows.

He drew long breaths and tried to get his bearings. Magic flames burned coldly in lanterns set on iron railings, and they cast a frigid blue light. Tiny ice crystals rimmed the lamps, and raindrops froze in curiously upward-jutting icicles.

He had arrived on the wrong side of town. Overcrowding was a problem in this district. When it wasn't raining, Immortals jammed the streets, and sometimes, when too many turned to shadow, the air became like a rising dark cloud. The residents here had poorly developed conjuring skills, if any, and relied on *servi*, to do their bidding. It was easier to kidnap someone from the realm of earth than to study and learn magic. Some Immortals had five or six *servi*, and, with land at a premium, they added rooms that projected out like balconies over the street.

Master Hawkwick lived a mile or so away, in a top-floor apartment with high turrets. Obie wondered what he was doing at that moment. He had received special dispensation from the Inner Circle, the assemble of the rulers in Nefandus, to teach Obie music. It had been for Hawkwick's enjoyment, but it had given Obie his passion. A strange homesickness came over him, but just when he considered stopping by his master's home, someone screamed overhead, and two shadows streaked from a window, wrestling each other and howling bitterly.

Any feelings of nostalgia deserted Obie. Living here had been a nightmare, but his memory seemed to have erased the bad and only retained the good. Maybe that was partly because it had been mandated that all *servi* had to remain drugged.

Obie couldn't linger; too many Regulators patrolled these twisting, narrow streets, and he had to find Berto. He stepped from his shelter, staying close to the building. He had only gone a short distance when running footsteps splashed into water somewhere behind him. His head snapped around, and, through the gray screen of rain, a dim figure sprinted toward him. He quickened his pace, and just as he started to turn the corner, someone grabbed his shoulders. Obie spun around and swung his fist, adrenaline surging through him. He didn't know how Regulators had found him so quickly, but they weren't taking him without a fight.

CHAPTER TWENTY

KYLE PUT UP HIS HANDS to defend himself, but Obie couldn't stop his punch. His knuckles slammed into Kyle's cupped palm with a loud *smack*.

"I thought you'd be happier to see me." Kyle smiled sheepishly. His clothes were soaked and plastered to his body. Water dripped from his nose and hair, and a curious smell of wet laundry surrounded him.

"You don't sneak up behind someone in a place like this," Obie complained, and shook out his fingers, trying to get rid of the sting. He could have really hurt Kyle. "How'd you get in here?"

"I hitched a ride with you." Kyle squinted

against the drenching rain. "But you ran off as soon as we got in. I've been looking for you ever since."

"You were the weight dragging on me," Obie said, understanding now why the passing had taken so dangerously long. It was always more difficult when someone was coming through with him. "Next time, let me know."

"Forget that," Kyle answered firmly. "I'll be using the portals from now on. I almost suffocated going through with you."

Obie started to explain but Kyle interrupted him. "I'm sorry," Kyle said, his voice almost inaudible in the pouring rain. "I thought about what you said. The three of us have to stick together. And instead of helping, my rules have been making us break apart."

"You're only trying to help," Obie said, feeling grateful for Kyle's apology.

"Thanks," Kyle said. "But right now we need to find Berto, rescue him and get him back without getting caught ourselves."

"I'm glad you followed me," Obie said and meant it.

"Someone had to come along and save your sorry butt," Kyle said jokingly. He smiled, and then his eyes became serious. "I want you to know I trust you. I must to follow you in here. I promised after my last visit that I'd never come back again."

"You visited here?" Obie asked, suddenly impressed.

They started walking, their feet slogging through puddles.

"Yeah," Kyle said. "I really hate this place."

They passed under shuttered windows and dark archways. The streets were deserted. Not even *servi* had ventured out in this tempest.

"If you hate it so much then why do you paint those pictures?" Obie asked finally.

Because I fell in love here," Kyle said. "With a goddess."

"She was that kind of pretty?" Obie asked.

"No, I mean she really was a goddess," he said. "I see her in Los Angeles still but she acts like she doesn't know me."

"Why?" Obie asked.

"She broke up with me because her father

is a member of the Inner Circle. She thought it was too dangerous for us to have a relationship." Kyle hurried ahead of him as if his heartbreak was still too painful and he didn't want to say more.

Obie followed after him, wondering if this was one of the secrets Berto had been talking about when they had spent the night under the Hollywood sign.

The street turned and turned again, becoming narrower, and with each turn, the waters deepened and ran more swiftly, carrying twigs, leaves, and an occasional discarded candle.

Rain hammered against Obie, but he felt lucky they had arrived during a bad storm. Few shape-shifters would venture out as shadows during heavy showers. They always claimed that afterward, when they materialized again, they felt as if the rain had thinned their blood. Such outings left them depleted for days.

Something splashed loudly behind them. Obie turned. Rain clattered on a line of tin barrels used to recycle trash, which meant dumping it in the earth realm, but he was certain that hadn't been the sound.

"Do you think they know we're here already?" Kyle asked, his eyes alert and nervous as if he had also heard something that didn't belong.

"Maybe." Obie studied the swirling and shifting currents, churning thick with debris now. He searched for a shadow form concealed within the mud. Not all Immortals hated water, and even those who did, might have found capturing two Renegades worth the risk.

Obie grabbed Kyle's arm and cautiously stepped back into a long alcove leading to a paneled door. The musky scent of mildew filled the air, and water dripped all around them. Obie caught movement out of the corner of his eye. He turned and studied the nebulous dark behind them. He didn't see anything that could pose a threat, but he couldn't shake the feeling that something had joined them

"Where does your aunt live, anyway?" Kyle asked, his voice echoing strangely in the small, enclosed space.

"The Other Side," Obie said, and caught the fleeting glimpse of terror on Kyle's face. The Immortals on the Other Side were masters of magic. Some were members of the Inner Circle. Power was centered among those who had had the strength to fight their way to the top of their vile and evil hierarchy.

Kyle let out a long, slow breath, as if he didn't think they had much chance of survival. "Let's get it over with, then."

Obie paused, trying to figure out which way to go. The streets here were like a maze, with too many dead ends and twisting alleys. He wanted to make sure they were heading in the right direction.

Finally, they started again, winding back the way they had come. A few blocks later an odd scratching sound made Obie turn. A gargoyle with a lapping tongue perched itself oddly on top of a scroll molding, staring down at him. Its mouth hung open, but no water spewed from it. The gutter might have been clogged, but Obie didn't see how one could have been connected to the funny, squat monster.

Something about the stone creature made him uneasy. He brushed the feeling away and ran to catch up with Kyle.

Less than a mile later, another scratching sound, like fingernails on blackboard, set Obie's teeth on edge. He stopped and listened more carefully. Beneath the burbling water, he clearly heard a rasp, followed by another crunch, as if someone were scraping bricks together. He shielded his eyes against the pelting rain and looked up. His mouth went dry and he held his breath. The same gargoyle with the lapping tongue sat on a lamppost, its body crusted with raindrops frozen by the cold flame, its demonic eyes glaring through the thin cover of ice. Now its skeletal body was exposed.

"The gargoyles." Kyle nudged him and pointed in a different direction. "On the roof over there."

Obie followed his look.

Three gargoyles had gathered on the conical spiral, their mouths open but not spewing water. They were jabbering to each other, sounding oddly like pigeons. Two more, with pointed ears and long snouts, gripped a chimney stack, their spindly stone talons clicking against the bricks. Another, the size of a cat, with bulging eyes and devil's horns, skulked along on the pitched roof, and tensed above the eaves, getting ready to pounce.

"Be careful," Obie said, stumbling backward.

"Like you needed to tell me that," Kyle said, and threw Obie a panicked look.

Suddenly the gargoyles sat up on their haunches, their stony eyes blinking, and they gazed fearfully at something farther down the street. Their gaping mouths released shrill, terrible screams. Then like a flock of startled birds, screeching and knocking against each other, they scampered across the steep rooftops, their granite claws clattering on the tiles, and vanished.

"What frightened them?" Obie asked, looking both ways, and then he knew. He clenched his jaw, backed up against the wall, and froze, certain his immortal existence would end here.

CHAPTER TWENTY-ONE

"IN HERE," OBIE WHISPERED, and he yanked Kyle's arm, pulling him behind the timber stairs. Obie peered out from between the balusters, and with a start, realized they were hiding near the building where Master Hawkwick lived. He looked up toward the third-floor apartment. The cone-shaped turrets disappeared into the low-hanging clouds, and the shutters were closed over the windows.

Two Regulators turned the corner and slogged through the flooded street, dragging their heavy legs. Obie's heart hammered crazily now, skipping too many thumps. Kyle began to shiver.

Regulators served the ancient evil enthroned in Nefandus. Its foul unholiness infected them, rotting their flesh and causing their monstrous appearance. When Regulators visited the earthly realm, they had the power to transform their bodies into movie-star perfection, but here they didn't bother, because their grotesqueness inspired dread.

They kept order with brutal force and sometimes chased Renegades between the two worlds. Usually that task was left to the *venatoris*, but Regulators still were the only ones who could execute Renegades. Obie had seen an execution once, and the terrible memory still haunted him. A Regulator had clasped a man tightly and absorbed his body, melting flesh and bone into its chest, taking the Immortal's spirit and life.

Obie's legs began to ache from sitting in one position, and his feet had started to fall asleep. He wiggled his toes to get the circulation back, and the wet sole of his tennis shoe squeaked on the tile.

The nearest Regulator twisted his head and stopped. He fixed his attention on the stairs. His fetid breath fumed over Obie and made it impossible to breathe.

Kyle had been trembling against Obie, but suddenly his body shifted, and Obie knew he now had a problem worse than not being able to breathe; Kyle intended to run.

Obie grabbed his wrist. "If you run, they'll catch you," Obie said in a terrified whisper. "You know what they'll do to you. Stay still, like you belong. Maybe they'll think we're newly arrived *servi* who've gotten lost."

At least Obie hoped that was what they would think. Kyle might know the outside world, but Obie was the expert here. It was common in this area to find newly abducted *servi*, vacant-eyed, shocked, and lost.

"I hate it here." Kyle moaned miserably, and then his lips continued moving in silent prayer.

"Make your mind as blank as you can."

Obie nudged him, and not for the first time wondered how Kyle had ever had the nerve to escape.

The first Regulator grunted, and the second one turned. His tiny black eyes were scaled over, but, through the milky pupils, he gazed at Obie and laughed until phlegm caught in his throat. He hacked, coughed, and spit.

Kyle had closed his eyes, as if it took all of his willpower to stay still. His hands were pressed flat against the wall behind him; he seemed unaware of the worms undulating over the gray bricks.

A sudden boom made the Regulators turn. Their attention was drawn away, probably to a fight between Immortals in another sector. They dissolved into inky smoke and soared into the storm, two jagged shadows making the rain steam.

"Okay," Obie said at last, hating the fear in his voice. "I'm sure they just thought we were new arrivals. They won't waste their time on us unless something else gives us away."

Obie started forward, and his heart

lurched. He stepped back quickly, knocking into Kyle, and pressed behind him, motionless.

Across the way, in the lashing rain, two figures detached themselves from the darkness near the arched entrance to the building. The silhouettes, one short and one tall, continued to materialize in the downpour. A large black umbrella wavered into shape over their heads.

"It's my master, Hawkwick," Obie whispered.

Hawkwick handed the umbrella to the girl with him.

"Who's the babe?" Kyle asked.

Obie snapped around. "We didn't come here to pick up girls."

"It's a simple question," Kyle answered angrily, but his testiness didn't fool Obie. His infatuation was obvious.

"Piya," Obie answered at last. "A *serva*."

Hawkwick stepped forward as if he had sensed a disturbance.

"Now you've done it," Obie whispered.

Raindrops spattered the lenses of

Hawkwick's wire-rimmed glasses. He took them off and squinted, obviously using a different kind of vision. A force pulsated from him, sparking in the rain, drifting thinly and circling into crevasses, snooping and searching the shadows and mists.

"Don't let him sense us," Obie warned, hunkering down. He squeezed against Kyle and tried hard to make his mind go blank again.

Hawkwick looked intently at the stairs where Obie and Kyle were hiding. The gaze shot through Obie, and his courage left him. He was surprised Hawkwick still had so much power over him. The need to go to him crawled unpleasantly through Obie.

Kyle clamped his hand over Obie's mouth, and only then did Obie realize he had been whimpering.

Then Piya coughed, her angelic face dripping rain, and Master Hawkwick walked swiftly back to her, his long cloak dragging in the water, and together they started up the iron stairs spiraling to the third floor. Piya carried a brown sack, with Hawkwick's favorite foods peeking over the top: Shake 'n Bake, Skittles, and Lay's Potato Chips.

Now Obie watched them climb the stairs, their footsteps echoing through the falling rain. At the top, Piya craned her neck over the railing, as if she were trying to catch sight of Obie, before she swept into the apartment and shut the door.

"We have to be more careful when we come back next time," Obie said.

"Next time?" Kyle didn't move. "No next time," he said firmly. "Never again."

They stayed in the hiding place for several minutes, afraid Hawkwick might be in the window high above them, looking down at the street.

"He's spooky," Kyle said and let a long sigh escape his lungs. "I thought there couldn't be anything worse than the Regulators who ran the digs." Many *servi* spent their days digging in the tunnels and mines throughout Nefandus.

"You haven't met my aunt yet," Obie said gloomily.

"I guess it's just my lucky day," Kyle

answered sarcastically, and then he stared vacantly as if he were viewing a memory. He glanced down at his hands. Rough orange calluses covered his palms. "What do you think they are looking for in the dig that they can't find by magic?"

"I don't know." Obie shook his head, still thinking about what had just happened. He had been frightened, but part of his fear had been of himself. Something inside him had wanted to go back to the life he'd had before. To drink the brownish drug and play the music, take the trips into the earth realm and listen to Master Hawkwick making fun of the people there. He hadn't been responsible then. Accountability was a blessing, but also a burden. He could take the credit for his own life now, but he also had to assume the blame.

Kyle nudged him, and they started forward again, not stopping to investigate sound or shadow, their pace quick and furtive.

Three miles away, Obie paused and stared at a gray stone house, set back from the road and surrounded by an iron fence. Fish-scale tiles covered a slanting roof that was over-crowded with pinnacles, turrets, and spires. The skull-shaped keystones over the dormer windows seemed alive, the hollow sockets glaring out. The evil atmosphere encircled him, bitterly cold and penetrating.

"That's my aunt Shatri's house," Obie said.

CHAPTER TWENTY-TWO

FOR A LONG TIME, OBIE and Kyle stood shivering beneath an overhanging honeysuckle branch. Through the sheeting rain, they watched the massive house. Primitive magic radiated from the masonry, coming off in waves, as if Shatri's home had absorbed her power and now released it in a protective shield.

"You think that's where Berto is?" Kyle asked, breaking their silence and not bothering to hide his reluctance to go inside.

"I'm positive she brought him here." Obie said, finally resolute, and trudged forward.

"Don't you think we should sneak up on the house?" Kyle asked, hanging back, his face pale, his lips bluish with cold.

"How?" Obie had the uncanny feeling that his aunt had been observing them all along. "She's too powerful not to be aware we're here. We'll go through the front door."

"Great," Kyle grumbled, started after him. "Hopefully, we won't get ourselves killed."

"Cheer up," Obie said glumly. "She can't kill us. We're immortal, remember?"

"In case you thought that would make me feel better, it didn't," Kyle said, he snorted. "If death were the worst thing she could do to us, it wouldn't be so bad."

"I know," Obie said, and stepped onto the stone walkway leading up to the door. Green moss covered the front porch. Obie took one step and cringed at the squishing sound his foot made on the slimy growth.

Kyle pulled back. "What is it?"

"A spell," Obie said. "If an unwanted visitor comes, the spines release poison."

"Then why didn't we turn to shadow and go in?" Kyle asked.

"I can't transform. Can you?" Obie said, his frustration matching Kyle's. "My blood is half adrenaline now."

"You're right." Kyle shook his head and mounted the steps.

"She kidnapped Berto. That was our invitation." Obie marched boldly forward, trying to hide his trembling. He crossed the porch and stopped at the door, taken aback by what he saw. The hilt of his father's sword now hung upside down, a door knocker. He blinked back hot tears, furious that his aunt could flaunt the murder of his father so blantantly. He touched the engraved metal, hoping to sense his father's spirit still lingering there.

"What now?" Kyle asked.

"This belonged to my father before—" Obie's throat closed around the words.

In anger he quickly inscribed the runic letters for "fire start." He knew that spell, from days of bivouacking with his father and the other warriors. Flames burst from the inscription, and the hilt fell from the knocker, glowing white-hot, then red. Obie waited for it to cool, his mind lost in prayer for the soul of his father.

Now was his chance to avenge the murder. He prayed to the Good in the universe to guide him, and then, with a jolt, he remembered that he stood on unsacred ground. He was in Nefandus.

When he looked up again, Kyle was marking the same runic letters for "fire start" over and over again on the door. Each time, he stepped back as if he expected an explosion of flames. It puzzled Obie that the inscription didn't work for Kyle.

"Maybe knowing how to do it isn't enough," Kyle said and looked at Obie strangely. "You probably have to be born with some kind of power."

"I don't know," Obie said. "It seemed like everyone in my family could do it."

"Maybe that's why you got the cushy job working with Master Hawkwick," Kyle muttered. "And I had to break my back digging."

"It's possible, I guess." Obie paused, wondering if there might have been another reason he had been given to Master Hawkwick. Could it be that Hawkwick had hoped to gain more than labor from Obie?

"How come no one's come to greet us?" Kyle asked, his voice heavy with trepidation.

In answer, the door swung open, and a force rushed around them as if a dozen hands with long, wiggling fingers pushed at their backs.

"I guess we have our greeting." Obie picked up the sword handle. The metal was still warm, and he remembered lifting it while it still retained the warmth of his father's hand.

Obie went first. Kyle followed him inside.

CHAPTER TWENTY-THREE

KYLE AND OBIE WALKED down the drafty entrance hall. Water dripped from their clothes and hair, pattering on the gleaming wooden floor. Flames set in lanterns lined the walls, and the cold, musty air rippled with golden light. But the glow didn't reach the far corners of the room. The vaulted ceiling stretched far above them, as if they stood at the bottom of a bell tower. Darkness hovered there, filled with murmuring voices.

Obie looked up and wondered if shape-shifters were overhead, deep in shadow, whispering to each other. He remembered the house and how haunted it felt. Memories awakened, fueling his hatred. His aunt had comforted him, grieved with him, and all along she had been his father's killer. The image of her leaning over him, shedding tears, burned bitterly in his mind.

But then his anger gave way to overwhelming guilt; he should have died with his father. He desperately wished he could travel back in time and return to that muggy afternoon when Shatri had attacked. If he had been there, maybe he could have changed the outcome, but he had been swimming and hadn't noticed his father's absence until it had been too late.

"Where should we go?" Kyle asked, interrupting his thoughts.

Obie looked around and sensed intuitively that they were supposed to follow the lamp fires. He started up the broad mahogany steps, and the flames blew out behind him.

His heart galloped, anticipating what might be waiting on the next floor. He curled his fingers tightly around the hilt of his father's sword and wished the heavy blade were still attached. But even such a powerful weapon would be no protection against his aunt; how did one slay an Immortal?

The staircase led up to a landing, then split and continued in two matching flights on either side to the next floor. Obie stopped. A prickling sensation crawled over the back of his neck. He couldn't shake the feeling that someone was watching him.

The muffled voices overhead became agitated, rising high. He could almost make out, words that seemed to be trying to warn him. He was certain the ghostly shadows weren't Followers. Abruptly the voices stopped, and quiet fell over Obie. Something had hushed whatever spirits were making the sounds. The deep silence was far worse.

Obie continued to the next landing, exhausted and feeling at the edge of his endurance. His emotions were stretched, and his back ached from shivering. The cold had leeched his strength.

In the upstairs hallway, only two of the many lanterns were lit, and those burned on either side of a closed door.

"He must be in there," Kyle said. He stopped a safe distance away.

"Or at least that's where we're supposed to go." Obie strode forward and turned the doorknob. His stomach clenched and his heartbeat thundered in his ears.

Kyle stood beside him, gritting his teeth, his breath coming in rapid gulps.

Together they peered inside.

Berto stood frozen in a large empty room, his eyes glazed and sightless. A yellow radiance shrouded his body, and the wispy letters of an incantation spun around him, imprisoning him in a binding spell as firmly as iron shackles. The iguana lay trapped beside him, caught in a globe of light, but the lizard fought against its captivity, claws grasping the fold of loose skin below its neck extended to scare its unseen enemy.

Obie and Kyle advanced slowly. The bloodred carpet absorbed their footfalls. Overhead hundreds of burning candles hung in chandeliers, but their yellow glow didn't cheer the atmosphere.

"I think Berto escaped the binding by projecting his spirit out," Obie said with renewed apprehension.

A silver thread left Berto's chest. It pierced the magic shield surrounding him, and fluttered into the room, looking like a single fiber from a spider web. The cord kept his spirit connected to his body when he did his dream walking.

"Doesn't he know how dangerous it is to do that astral projection here?" Kyle said. "Anything could take possession of his body while his spirit's gone."

"Maybe if we turned to shadow we could follow the cord, find his spirit and bring him back." But even as Obie spoke, he knew his nerves were too jangled to make his body fade and he didn't think Kyle could either.

Suddenly, the flames sputtered in the chandeliers and a fountain of sparks whirled into the air, crystallizing into the silhouette of a woman. Shatri stepped from the luminous cloud, her movements as smooth as a viper's. Her hair, pale blue now, floated around her in a halo, and her face was iridescent like an angel, the dangerous kind. She seemed taller than Obie remembered, and more lethal, her eyes snake green. A glossy white gown, spangled with pearls and diamonds, clung to her, the hem swirling around her delicate feet.

"Omer," she said. "I'm so glad you accepted my invitation and brought a friend."

"As if I had a choice," Obie said obstinately, and glared at his aunt. Even though her manner was charming, he felt something deeply unpleasant about her.

She brushed her hand over his cheek in a friendly greeting, but before she could kiss him, he recoiled. Her fingers had felt like a serpent slithering over his skin.

"You're cold," she said. "We'll have tea."

The double doors swooshed open behind them, revealing a grand parlor, and the smells of freshly baked scones and vanilla tea cakes wafted around them.

Kyle let out a dry whistle and moved closer to Obie.

A scrawny girl, with drug-induced saucer eyes, flapped a scarlet cloth over the table near the fireplace and began setting the tea service from a cart. A second *serva* with short fluffy hair ran across the plush carpet, carrying two purple tunics. She offered them to Obie and Kyle.

"It's what my *servi* wear," Shatri said, turning. "But it's better than shivering."

She went into the parlor as if she expected them to change their clothes right there. Immortals disregarded the need for privacy of people from the earth realm, as if they thought all *servi* were possessions without needs, other than minimal shelter, feed, and water.

"It's better than freezing," Obie said and peeled off his shirt, then slipped the tunic over his head, before sliding off his sopping tennis shoes, socks, jeans, and underwear. He took the helle rune from his jeans pocket and slipped it into the front pouch on his tunic, then clasped the handle of his father's sword again.

Kyle struggled to fit into his gown. When

he finished, he looked down at his exposed knees and shook his head. "If we get out of this, you owe me big time."

"Mine's shorter." Obie was taller than Kyle, and his tunic only came to mid-thigh. He started into the parlor, but when he glanced back to see if Kyle was following him, he realized his mistake. The *serva* with the fluffy hair was already walking away with their clothes. If they escaped now, they would have to wear the tunics, and any Regulator who saw them would be suspicious and not automatically assume they were new arrivals who had become lost.

Obie joined his aunt, and sat down. He thumped the sword handle on the table in accusation.

"You've broken my door knocker." Shatri smiled devilishly and tried to take it back.

Obie grabbed it first and slipped it into his pouch.

"If you had only cooperated, Omer," she said, pouring tea. "Your life in Nefandus could have been quite different from the one you suffered. Look at the splendor in which you could have lived. I would have shared everything with you and still will."

"Is that why you wanted me back?" he asked bitterly. "You're lonely and need someone to comfort you?"

She ignored his question and handed him a cup of tea. The flowery jasmine fragrance steamed over his face, and soothed his rage. His mouth watered, anxious to savor the brew, he started to sip and stopped. The tea must contain a drug or be cursed with a spell. He glanced at Kyle. He was already drinking.

"Don't," Obie shouted, and marked the air with a runic inscription for *break*. Immediately, the windows crashed. Mirrors and china shattered. Glass spun around the room. Hot tea spilled across the table, dripping onto the carpet, and wind rushed in, splattering rain. The curtains billowed out, twisting wildly. The *servae* screamed in terror and ran from the room.

Obie winced, wondering what Shatri would do to him now.

"Omer," she said as if he were a child, her laughter ringing sweetly. She waved her hand with a flourish, marking a spell. Gold light trembled from her fingers, growing larger, then whisked about the room

The windows and mirrors came back together, and the broken porcelain reassembled with the tea still twirling inside. Calm returned. Kyle stared blankly at Obie and left his cup on the table.

"If you had inherited any magic from your mother," Shatri went on as if nothing had happened. "You would have known the tea was free of pollutants." She studied him now as she often had when he was young.

He had thought then that she had looked at him with love and pity, but now, he clearly saw the disdain and puzzlement in her eyes.

"I put a curse on you the night you were born," Shatri said softly. "You should have only lived until your mother's campfire burned out."

Obie was stunned, and remained silent, contemplating her words.

"I've never had a spell fail me, before or since. I thought perhaps you had been born with some great power that prevented me from killing you. When I could find nothing special in you, I gave you to Hawkwick, but he found even less. Now, I can see for myself that you have no gift, so what magic did your mother cast that night that made, Hel, the goddess leave you with life?"

"I told you, Shatri," a familiar voice said behind Obie. "The only spell I cast was love."

Obie turned and forgot to breathe. His mother stood behind him.

CHAPTER TWENTY-FOUR

DEEP INSIDE, OBIE FELT like crying and screaming, but he stoically pushed back his emotions and stood, knocking over the chair. His mother had none of the blackness he had seen in the eyes of other *draugr*. She couldn't be one of the living dead, and yet she stood before him, alive in death, more beautiful even than his memories of her. She wore a white gown with ancient lettering embroidered across the bodice. Her hair flowed over her shoulders in thick braids, and she still wore the love amulet his father had clasped around her neck the day they buried her. She opened her arms in the most natural way and Obie ran to her.

He nestled against her and caught the scent of dark sorcery in her hair, then he felt the welts on her arms and pulled back. He stood close to her now, and could clearly see the runic inscriptions burned into her arms and forehead. The Haliurunnae had engaged in magic with the world of the dead. One of them must have taught his aunt Shatri how to entrap his mother's spirit and bring her back to life.

"I fought Shatri, hoping she wouldn't be able to force you to come to Nefandus," his mother whispered. "And at the same time I longed to see you again."

"Why did she do this to you?" Obie said, trying to quell his tears. He had anticipated danger and possibly enslavement again, but he hadn't been prepared to find his mother this way.

"After centuries of searching, Shatri found my rune stones," his mother answered. "She had hoped that if she conjured me I would show her how to use their magic."

His mother's voice was soothing and strong, but the terrible weariness in her eyes frightened him. Could a spirit die?

"Silence!" Shatri glared at his mother and worked her fingers as if trying to cast a spell to keep her from talking. Light sputtered and crackled, prickling the air, until a cloud imbued with broken incantations circled Shatri. Then, as if she had remembered one last hex, her hand snapped up and made a slash. The clamor of pounding drums and hellhounds breaking loose filled the room. The air blurred, then split apart as a thick black shadow eased through the crack and raced toward them.

Obie's mother lifted her arm and redirected the spell. The grimy haze circled Kyle. He shouted, flinched, and froze.

"Don't worry about your friend," Obie's mother said. "I diluted Shatri's spell. It won't hold him long."

Obie hoped that was true, but his mind quickly turned to other concerns. He touched the sword handle in his pouch. "Did Shatri kill my father because she wanted the rune stones?"

"No," his mother answered and looked at her sister. "Shatri was passionately in love with your father. She wanted him for herself alone, but he never wanted her and the only way she could possess him was to kill him."

"But who won in the end?" Shatri asked angrily, her eyes narrowed to fierce slits. "You have nothing, Lisha, not even your spirit. I control it and now I have your son as well."

"You'll never convince him to join you," Obie's mother said, clasping the love amulet hanging around her neck. "And I still have the one thing you want: King Filimer's eternal love."

"We'll see." Shatri smirked and flicked her wrist. Strange letters bubbled in the air and grew, spreading into a thin vapor. The gray tendrils seeped slowly toward Obie and his mother.

Shatri walked across the room, her hem fluttering over the red carpet. She sat in front of a desk near an arched window, opened a drawer, and pulled out a small leather pouch that had once belonged to Obie's mother.

"Come, Omer," Shatri said, her voice inviting. "Let me at least show you the rune stones."

Obie glanced at his mother. She stood entranced now within a fine fog, her arms twitching as if she were fighting the spell. Her eyes frantically shifted back and forth, trying to communicate something. Her lips trembled and she mouthed *go*. He assumed she wanted him to go to Shatri.

Reluctantly, he left his mother and marched to where his aunt sat. He took a chair near her, then looked back, wondering what enchantment controlled his mother now.

"This has gone on too long," Shatri said softly, as if she didn't want the others to hear. "We would have had this over long before now, but every time I tried to summon you, your mother stopped me. She was stronger in death than I had anticipated. She even managed to send a wind song to hover over you and deflect my spells. I'm sure you've felt us fighting. So much wasted energy, when all I needed was the tiniest favor. Help me and then you're all free to go with my blessing."

Obie nodded, suddenly wondering why he had made such a fuss. It really had been foolish not to grant Shatri her wish. He could see that clearly now.

Shatri shook out the pouch. Small gray stones clattered onto the desktop and rolled about. Her long fingers arranged them in a spell for friendship. Normally, a pinkish halo would have surrounded everyone in the room and made them forget their animosities, but now nothing happened.

"You see?" Shatri shrugged prettily, and cocked her head. "I don't know how to work your mother's runes. It's an embarrassment to me." She pushed them closer to Obie, making a soft scraping sound. "Show me how. Just one little spell."

"That's all?" Obie asked, wanting to help her. He knew how to arrange simple incantations, like the spell for finding water for his horse, but he wasn't sure if he could remember now.

Shatri began turning the stones blank side up. "If you don't trust me, then ask the oracle in the runes. Draw one, and the symbol chosen will tell you what to do."

Many members of his tribe had consulted the runes for advice and guidance, but even if he did take one, when he turned it over to read the letter, would he know what it signified? He tapped the table, wishing he knew more.

Unexpectedly, Kyle broke free from his trance and staggered over to them, his steps unsure and lopsided, as if some other force were dragging him forward.

"What does she want?" Kyle asked, his eyes blinking away his drowsiness.

"She brought me back to Nefandus to show her how to use my mother's runes," Obie said. "All she wants is for me to cast one spell."

"Do it," Kyle said, suddenly animated. "Do it and let's get out of here."

Obie reached out but as he started to pick up a stone, a slender hand clasped his fingers and stopped him. His mother stood over him, looking worn, as if fighting Shatri had drained her spirit. "Your touch will awaken the power in the runes that died when I died," she warned.

Shatri looked up, startled, and huffed, then growled something under her breath.

"Shatri has hypnotized you both," his mother scolded gently, and waved her hand in front of his eyes, then she did the same to Kyle.

Obie shook his head. Kyle looked stunned.

"Then why did you tell me to go to her," Obie asked, terrified of what he had almost done.

"I mouthed *no*," his mother answered.

"Do what I ask!" Shatri slapped the desk. "Or your mother will remain my *serva*, and I will send your friends back to the digs to labor forever."

Obie couldn't condemn his mother or his friends to an eternity of servitude. He scooped the stones into his hands. "I'm sorry," he yelled. "There's no other way."

Shatri grinned, triumphant, and reached for the runes.

CHAPTER TWENTY-FIVE

OBIE STARTED TO HAND the runes to Shatri. "First, give me your promise to free my mother and friends," he said, impatient to be rid of the curiously cold bits of rock. The stones trembled, awakening from a long hibernation, and squirmed unpleasantly against his skin.

"Stop, Omer." His mother grabbed his wrist, alarmed. "You're the rune master now."

"How can I be?" Obie asked. "I can barely remember what you taught me, and what I do remember is wrong."

His mother released her grip and in the same moment a white-hot light circled his hands. The rune stones burned his palms, branding their letters into his skin. He screamed in pain, then held his breath as the fire seared up his arms. He stepped back, closer to the hearth, and leaned against the wall. The intense heat spread through him, ravaging muscle and bone, and just when he could endure no more, the agony turned into something welcome and desired.

A pristine power raced over him, sheathing his body with ancient and sacred illumination. Again he cried out, but not from pain this time, he felt overwhelmed and wanted to celebrate the blessed mystery that had given him life.

He was vaguely aware of Shatri screaming foul words, and of his mother watching him with love and pride. Kyle hovered close by, as if waiting for a chance to rescue him from the strange glow, but Obie didn't want to be saved from this radiance; it was saving him.

The primordial force strengthened his spirit, leaving him exalted and resolute, and willing to die for the magic that empowered the runes, and with his unspoken pledge, the fragrance of burning roses swept through him. The delicate taste tingled in his mouth and throat. He blinked as a peculiar dizziness made him gasp for air.

Obie shook his head. He sensed the evil from Nefandus stalking deep inside him, ravenous and eagerly waiting for a chance to overwhelm him, but now he possessed an equally strong strength of purity.

He looked at Shatri. "I'll never surrender the runes to you," he said firmly.

"Let's get out of here," Kyle whispered as if he sensed increasing danger.

Shatri tromped across the carpet to a far corner, her rancor like a bitter cloud, filling the room with terrible foreboding. She picked up her staff. The rich, dark wood seemed lustrous, and then Obie realized the gleam was caused by the endlessly moving runic symbols running up and down the slender pole. He could feel the energy building.

"You must go now, Omer. Leave!" His

mother screamed. "You have the runes. Go back to the world and fulfill your destiny."

But before she could finish her warning, Shatri aimed her staff at Obie, and discharged a thunderbolt, making the walls shook. The surrounding area became saturated with the stench of death and graves.

Obie's mother flung out her hand. A glowing ball burst loudly forth, chasing after the streaking light. Electrical veins crackled from it and imprisoned Shatri's attack. Flames erupted, twining around each other. The two forces battled, scattering sparks, then a spear of brightness burst free and shrieked at Obie, gathering speed. He ducked too late, and prepared for the pain. The light screeched at him and struck the pouch of his tunic, hitting the handle of his father's sword. The impact knocked him back but wasn't as perilous as it might have been. Black embers spiraled around him and he wobbled forward, his tunic smoldering. He breathed the circling cinders and the dank taste of caves and illness slid over his tongue.

Shatri aimed again.

Obie dove recklessly under the table and banged his head on the pedestal. The impact jarred through him, and his hands opened. The rune stones bounced and scattered across the rug. In the semiconscious state, he suddenly knew what to do. Still stunned, he pulled himself up to his knees and frantically began looking for the stones.

Kyle lunged next to him and tried to pull Obie to safety.

"Get the runes!" he shouted, yanking away from Kyle. "Before Shatri can."

Both Obie and Kyle threw themselves at the same stone, and butted heads.

Obie moaned and rolled over, slumping to his side. He struggled to his hands and scrambled forward, his head throbbing fiercely. He gathered three and tried to remember how many stones were in the set. He thought the number was thirty-five, but how were they going to collect so many before Shatri shot another magic bolt?

"Hurry!" he shouted in panic.

"Like you needed to tell me that!" Kyle

answered heatedly, picking up another stone.

In Obie's peripheral vision he became aware of his mother, fearlessly moving into position to confront Shatri.

"Get the stones!" Shatri shoved her *servae*. The girl with the fluffy hair ran over to Obie and clawed at his clenched fists, her eyes twitching as if terrified to displease her master. The other jumped on his back, screaming into his ear, her small hands slapping his face.

Obie brushed them away and stood. He counted twenty stones in his hands. He looked anxiously at Kyle. "How many do you have?"

"I have fourteen," Kyle shouted, and flinched as Shatri stomped closer, swinging her staff. Light flashed from the end, erupting into arrows that shot at them.

Kyle quickly transferred the stones into Obie's cupped hands.

"One more!" Obie screamed, and then he saw *eihwaz* precariously perched on the edge of the hearth. He dove to the ground and reached for it as a blazing light stabbed his arm, cutting through skin to muscle. The air around him filled with the stench of burning flesh and he slouched, inches from the last rune, his arm dead at his side.

But Obie had once seen a warrior fight with his dying breath, one arm severed, and the other arm swinging a sword and taking his enemy into to death with him. Obie could be as valiant now. He stretched and grasped the stone. His fingers fumbled and he dropped it once, then picked it up, and on his knees, he turned to face Shatri as if he were surrendering the stones.

He bowed before her, but as he did, he arranged the runes in a hiding spell, a game he remembered playing with his mother as a boy.

The room became eerily quiet.

"No!" Shatri shouted when she realized what he was doing, but her stopping charm was too slow.

The runes vanished.

"What did you do?" Kyle asked, frustration rising in his voice. "The stones were our only hope."

"I couldn't let her have their magic," Obie said, resigned. "And I never had enough skill to combat her sorcery. I'm sorry."

Shatri directed her staff at Kyle. A bolt knocked him against the wall and he hit his head with a heavy thud. She pointed at Obie, then paused, letting the magical energy grow.

An eerie silhouette filled the space behind her, radiating a purple glow.

Obie's mother sprinted toward Shatri, her face a grimace of pain as she forced herself forward against Shatri's dark magic. Her fingers discharged rainbow lights of counterspells. Bright illumination circled the room but did nothing to stop Shatri this time.

Defenseless and languishing, Obie bravely prepared to meet his fate. He was an Immortal. Shatri couldn't kill him, but he had learned from living in Nefandus that there were fates worse than death.

CHAPTER TWENTY-SIX

AT FIRST, OBIE WASN'T sure whose ghostly image stood behind Shatri, but then the apparition glided closer and he saw Berto smile slyly. His dream-walking spirit clutched Shatri's staff and yanked hard, misdirecting the charge. The beam catapulted into the wall and a loud boom ricocheted around the room. Flames lashed out and tendrils of fetid smoke curled to the ceiling.

Shatri twisted around, surprised. But before Berto could steal her staff, she flicked her free hand. Arcane letters stained the air, pausing briefly before pelting Berto and tattooing his illusory form with charms. He soared backward as if the silver thread connecting his soul to his physical self were rewinding at lightning speed. Through the double doors, Obie saw Berto slam back into his body.

The distraction lasted long enough for Obie to pull himself to his feet. Then he plunged forward and grabbed Shatri's staff. The wood secreted magic and it seeped over his fingers like slime. His legs felt too weak to hold him, and dizziness made it hard to concentrate, but he threw his head back and let out a yell. His battle cry rang around him, empowering him, and he wrenched the unholy staff from Shatri.

He clasped the long pole tightly, and broke it over his knee. He started to throw the two pieces aside, but a deep roar came from the broken halves, vibrating violently in his hands. Blue flames licked the ends and then runic letters burst from the break, spilling over Shatri. Incantations shot forth and impaled her. She screamed and her hands worked frantically, wildly casting bindings to counteract her own magic.

The hieroglyphs squiggled over her face and arms until an evil mosaic covered her, and then the letters began to burn. Her hair swept up in a blazing whirlwind. Her skin crinkled beneath the flames. Her face became corpse-like, eyes dead, and after that she dissolved.

Obie stepped back. A freezing breeze wafted around him and his lungs filled with the horrible stench of dark magic. Shatri was gone. Only ash remained, shifting on the wood floor near the carpet.

"That's it?" Kyle stepped beside Obie, looking down. "Just like that, she's gone."

"I hope so," Obie said, feeling disoriented and ill. He coughed and spit the cold foul air from his lungs.

Berto joined them. His binding spell had been broken when Shatri turned to ash. He cradled the iguana and touched the cinders with his toe. The gray powder swirled. Grains slid over each other, and drifted as if trying to get away.

"All her spells should be broken," Obie's

mother whispered. "I should have been released when she turned to dust."

Obie stared at his mother. She looked exhausted, her eyes frightened, but worse, Shatri's malevolent markings still scared her arms and forehead. What would happen to her spirit now?

"We'll take your mother with us," Kyle said abruptly. "We'll find someone who'll know what to do."

Obie's mother nodded. "Shatri's ashes contain too much power to be left here. We need to take them back and inter them in a burial mound."

"I don't want to touch her," Kyle said.

"Shatri was an Immortal." Berto handed the iguana to Obie. "She'll start regenerating if we don't do something." He peeled off his T-shirt and knelt down. Tiny dust devils formed, fighting his touch, but he carefully swept the residue into his shirt, then rolled it tight.

"We need to get out of here before someone else finds us," Kyle said anxiously, then paused and looked at Obie. "Unless you can take us."

"No way," Obie said. His mouth felt dry and his throat clicked. He wondered why he still felt so afraid.

"We'd better hurry," Berto said, looking down at his wristwatch. The face showed earth's changing night sky. "The portal opens soon."

They ran into the dim hallway. Kyle led. Obie held his mother's arm and Berto carried the iguana. The shadows moved around them, billowing out and growing. The whispering they had heard earlier grew louder, then something cold and gossamer hit Obie's face. He swatted at it, thinking cobwebs had stretched over him, but whatever it was grabbed back, licking tightly around his wrist.

In the same moment, Berto sucked in air.

"What is it?" Kyle yelled, his hands slapping as if fighting an invisible attack.

"You mean, what are they?" Berto said, breathless, and pointed.

A chorus of women stood beside him, their

hair writhing around their faces. Black runic letters cut deep into their foreheads and arms. They glared at Obie with savage hatred, their eyes fiery with vindictiveness, as if he were the one who had called their spirits forth from death. More materialized, bobbing in the air, their voices burbling.

"Great." Kyle looked at Obie. "You got rid of the queen witch, but now you've summoned her minions."

"They can't be bad," Obie said. "They're the ones who were whispering and trying to warn us on our way in."

"Then why are they looking at us like that?" Kyle said, easing closer to Obie and Berto.

"Because they want their freedom," Obie's mother answered as if it were her own desire. "They're the Haliurunnae. Shatri enslaved their spirits, just as she did mine."

"It's dangerous to conjure the dead," Berto said. "Because they have to kill their master to gain their freedom, and since you took out Shatri, I think they're after you."

"We freed you!" Kyle shouted. "You can go home now."

But the women slipped closer and slowly surrounded them. Obie could smell the death and magic misting off their bodies, and now he saw why they couldn't speak loudly. Ancient incantations scrolled over their lips, quieting their voices. He imagined that their shrieking and wailing had annoyed Satri.

"Use your runes and release them," Obie's mother said quickly. "Or they'll possess your bodies to escape Nefandus."

"That's the thing," Kyle said, irritably. "Obie made the runes vanish so Shatri couldn't have them."

"I can call them back." Obie waved his hand and the runes tumbled from the air, clattering into his hands.

"Do something then!" Kyle said impatiently.

"Do what?" Obie answered. "Shatri studied dark magic. I know how to make a frog lead me to water. I don't think that's going to help us now."

"Think," Berto whispered. "You must know how to cast a spell to help us now. Try anything."

"You've always had the power," his mother encouraged. "Try."

Obie knelt and scattered the runes on the floor in front of him. He held his breath, concentrating. His mother had given him an inscription for protection. He had written it on his arm, but it had been one to protect him from temptation, not from an attack of evil *draugr*. Maybe it could work now on the living dead. He nervously arranged the stones. Nothing happened.

"Try again!" Kyle yelled, and stepped back.

"Remember what your father taught you," his mother said. "Trust your intuition."

The women shrieked over Kyle, their voices blending into an ungodly sound. Kyle thrashed about, trying to fight them, but then his eyes locked in a dreamy vacant stare. Berto had the same glazed look, but his trance could have been self-induced.

Obie didn't understand why the women

weren't attacking him, and then he remembered the helle rune. He pulled it from his pouch. Inna might have been a sorceress but she had never been evil. This stone was used by necromancers. He sensed it had the power to release his mother's spirit and return the Haliurunnae to the restful dead.

He glanced up. One of the women had turned to vapor, and was seeping slowly around Kyle as if she were about to possess him.

Obie dropped the helle rune into his spread. Now he had a cast of thirty-six stones. He waited impatiently.

A light began to grow from the runes. It swept out and circled the women. At once, the inscriptions on their skin began to fade. Their fury and hatred gave way to peaceful sighs. Kyle and Berto were freed from their trances.

Obie turned abruptly. The spell was also working on his mother.

"There's so much I need to tell you so you can be safe." His mother reached out, struggling to stay with him. "Destiny is waiting for you. You must fulfill the Legend. It's the only way you'll be able to return home to your own time and live out a normal life. Each of you is a channel through which the Good in the universe can flow, and together . . ." she stopped. "Where is the fourth?"

Berto shook his head. "It's just us."

"Four must come together . . ." she insisted.

"The Legend?" Obie said urgently sensing his mother didn't have much time. "Tell us the Legend."

"Go forth," she whispered, and signed a blessing with her fingers.

Obie tried to hold onto her but it was like grasping a breeze. She vanished. He stared at the wavering air. Was her spirit at peace now, resting with his father? Or was she nearby guarding him?

Berto grabbed his arm and pulled him out the door. "Don't think about her now," he whispered. "Concentrate on getting out of here, and then later you can mourn."

Outside, rain hit Obie with reviving force. He splashed through puddles after Kyle and

Berto, the iguana bobbing in his arms. This time he ignored the raven-black darkness hovering around him.

"Dive!" Kyle yelled suddenly. "The portal's closing!" He threw himself at a wall. It looked as if he was going to smash his head against the bricks and then he disappeared. Berto dove in after him, passing through the structure. Obie started to leap but before he could, two Regulators materialized in front of him. A corona of sparks flickered around their monstrous heads.

CHAPTER TWENTY-SEVEN

OBIE STOPPED AND swallowed hard, trying to quell his stomach. More than anything he wanted to return to Los Angeles. He concentrated, clutching the iguana tightly, and tried to open the boundary between the two worlds. Soon his vision blurred and his surroundings became distorted. The rainy night buckled and fractured. The Regulators stretched and then compressed into bizarre geometric shapes.

A delicate membrane enveloped Obie and

his body became numb as his atoms reconfigured. Then, without warning, a dull ache spread through him, and he fell back into Los Angeles. Bright sunshine wrapped around him and he let out a whoop.

Kyle and Berto waited for him on the sidewalk, still dripping rainwater. Berto was barechested, his T-shirt with Shatri's ash rolled under his arm. Kyle's tunic looked like a dress. A large knot bulged on his forehead.

Obie started to laugh, then realized he looked just as weird. His purple tunic was scorched, sopping wet, and only reached to mid-thigh, plus he cradled an iguana.

"It feels good to be home," Obie said and started walking back to the apartment. His choice of words surprised him. It was the first time he had called Los Angeles his home.

Late that evening, Obie, Kyle, and Berto carried Shatri's remains to the La Brea Tar Pits on Wilshire Boulevard. They circled the black bog in front of the George C. Page Museum, the smell of tar heavy in the air. The museum had closed but the security guards didn't seem concerned when Obie, Kyle and Berto climbed the grassy slope that covered the walls of the building.

"You're right," Obie said. "From the back, the museum does looks like a burial mound."

"I hope burying her here is enough to contain her power," Kyle said, but he looked doubtful.

Berto pulled the spade from his jacket pocket, kneeled and carefully took out the sod, then Obie took a hand shovel and together they dug.

When the hole was deep enough, Obie took a felt marker and wrote a runic inscription across the material to prevent Shatri from rising again, but as he set the bundle in the grave, an odd chill passed through his body. "I know my mother said to bring her back and bury her, but—"

"Her ashes were too powerful to leave in Nefandus," Kyle interrupted.

Berto put the sod in place, then he pointed to the frieze on the square roof of the building at the top of the hill. "The carvings of the saber-toothed tigers and mammoths are powerful magic. They'll help keep her spirit contained."

"Let's go." Kyle started down the incline with Berto.

Obie ran after them, suddenly remembering something that pushed his other worries aside. "Hey Berto, can I borrow your cell phone?"

"Sure." Berto dug into his pocket and handed Obie the phone. "Who do you need to call?"

Obie didn't answer, but just smiled. He held the phone in his hand and looked at it intently, waiting for something to happen.

"Man, you got to dial the phone first." Berto grabbed it back. "Magic doesn't work here."

Berto gave Obie a lesson in calling information, and then showed him how to punch in the number.

Obie's heart hammered against his chest. He took a deep breath while the line rang. "Hello, Beckman Guitar Shop."

"Hey," Obie said, trying hard to sound casual.

"I was hoping you'd call," Allison said and the happiness in her voice made him think he might be able to adjust to life here after all.

He glanced up at the clear Los Angeles sky as he walked to the car talking to Allison, and for an instant he heard a wind song, playing hauntingly above him. He sensed his mother's spirit within the notes, somewhere in the heavens smiling down on him.

DON'T MISS THE NEXT BOOK,

escape